THEATRE OF INCEST

Library of Congress Cataloging-in-Publication Data

Arias-Misson, Alain.
Theatre of incest / by Alain Arias-Misson. -- 1st ed.
p. cm.
ISBN-13: 978-1-56478-481-0 (alk. paper)
ISBN-10: 1-56478-481-9 (alk. paper)
1. Incest--Fiction. I. Title.
PS3551.R43T47 2007
813'.54--dc22
2007026631

www.dalkeyarchive.com

Printed on permanent/durable acid-free paper
and bound in the United States of America

THEATRE OF INCEST

 ALAIN ARIAS-MISSON

DALKEY ARCHIVE PRESS
Champaign · London

For Karen

My mother my lover
My daughter my other
My sister my sweet witch

Part I

❧   MY MOTHER MY LOVER   ❧

Entrance Window

When, as a child, I first caught sight of my mother naked, I thought she was being punished. The rain was beating on the roof of my troubled dreams, and the thunder roaring, raging. I was frightened. My bedroom window looked out across the long driveway into the trees, and it was dark, the trees quaking like ghosts. I wanted my Mother, I wanted to pee. I began crying and got out of bed, wandering down the dark corridor and then along the balcony that looked down into the living room, Mummy! Mummy! But my voice was smothered by the storm and the howling wind. Then a flash lit up everything like bright day and I saw them below for an instant, both pale and raw-looking. My father was doing something terrible to my mother, humping and jerking on top of her, and she was crying and groaning. I was filled with amazement. Then I went back to bed very quietly, although I wanted my Mother even more than before. I lay awake for a long time but I was no longer frightened of the storm.

The Entrance Toilet Window

When I was only about four or five, Melle, as my mother called her (for "Mademoiselle"), a stocky, tough, mustachioed Frau, raised me to face level and swilled my little penis about in her mouth with some gusto. Melle was German. My mother had been raised by her. Perhaps it is to this premature act that I owe my special predilection? Or perhaps not. Of course I was quite helpless in her muscular grip, but I have no reason to think that I wanted to resist this tender rape. On the contrary. But Melle was a hard, dominant old bitch. And what was my mother's attitude in all this (she certainly suspected something)? Approval, I guess. Or at least understanding.

Father's Bedroom Window

The first time I wore my mother's silk panties, they were much too big, they kept slipping off—my little penis was stiff and they slid down over, and I would pull them up again, exacerbating the sweetness. I had deliberately avoided looking in the tall closet mirror, and would only just peek at myself prancing out there, doubled, just glancing out of the corner of my eye so that I—I mean I in the mirror—wouldn't appear to notice that I was watching. And I out there in the room, pretended not to see either, hardly turning my head, so that both of us seemed not to be watching the other, and I could see me as I really was, almost without anything of myself being involved. I forgot the other me with the slithery sweet touch of the panties about my bottom and between my thighs, stroking my little balls like feathery fingers. I danced and skipped so that the panties would slip off by accident and I would be revealed, and then I pretended not to see myself out there with the same stiff little penis watching me, and I'd look away quickly. Of course I had to come back and forth again each time, otherwise I would go off the edge, and I couldn't go beyond this invisible barrier either. Now I knew how Mummy must feel her softness inside. Soon my cock and balls became moist with the silky caress of the panties and I could hardly breathe, and the mirror cracked! No, it was the door that opened in the mirror! I couldn't move. I heard a light laugh tinkling, and the door closed again. I took off the panties in a rush, not easy because they were tangled and wet with my penis, which stayed hard despite my shame, and I ran to the closet drawer and stuffed them back where I found them, and gave one last look at the big mirror and saw myself, funny-looking, very small, naked, white-faced, my penis still sticking out. But why didn't she come to spank me? How long did she watch, I wondered with a thrill of panic.

Window of Main Bathroom

I was jealous of the men who knew her when she was twenty-seven. I felt they had taken unfair advantage of me. I had worn her panties and wet them, but it wasn't enough. I wanted more. I remember watching her when she prepared the blankets on the playroom floor for my afternoon nap. I watched as she bent over and her skirt rode high up her legs and I could see her tender thighs resplendent in the white stockings, almost all the way up, to where the white stopped and the darkness of her groin began.

And when I lay down in my bed and pretended to sleep, and she came over to see if I was asleep, I would glance up quickly when she turned away and glimpse her white-pantied crotch for an instant. Whenever I got a chance I spied on her. I saw her sometimes through the keyhole of the bathroom. Once I saw her completely naked, but all I could look at was the dark cluster of hair at her pubic mound. I was amazed at it, it seemed to belong to an alien world. I watched it, she walked back and forth as if on show for me, and I could examine it very closely, a furry animal that didn't altogether belong to my mother. One time, I must have made some noise because she suddenly looked right at the keyhole as if she could see me. After that, whenever I tried to look through the keyhole, to my disappointment and frustration there was something on the other side blocking the view. I realized of course this meant that she knew I knew. And curiously, while that shared consciousness embarrassed me, it also created a thrill of anxiety. I of course didn't know about fucking. I just knew that it had to do with that thing between her legs. I only had the following two pieces of information: when the boys were in music class and we sang an old children's song, "I'm looking over a four leaf clover . . ." we would substitute other words, "First come the ankles, then come the knees, next comes the bush—" and something about "between the trees." I could never remember or "get" the next line, but I knew it concerned the secret of the furry crotch she had displayed. But what would it feel like if you put your hand in there: that was my preoccupation. The other information I had was the explanation proffered by a little companion, that the man puts his thing inside her thing. The graphic idea horrified me and I had to stop thinking about it.

Second Window of Main Bathroom

She sat me on the bidet and washed my penis thoroughly until it stood out "like a little soldier," she said laughing, and leaned down, her large head of reddish hair spilling about, veiling the sacrificial feast. Then she drew me to my feet, took me to the bed and pulled me on top of her. I was barely an adolescent, I didn't know how to do it. I pretended

I did but was imprisoned in all her straps and clasps and belts and hooks and hasps, I rolled on top of her trying to get in but it was a complicated machinery and I didn't understand how it all worked, which bits came apart and which stayed on, what was I supposed to do? I wallowed about on this sleek expanse of white flesh that I lusted for and didn't know how to get into! Finally, despairing of me, she just englobed me between her thighs, swallowed me into her body. I was lost in this dark sea, perhaps I would drown, I thought, and I swam out farther and farther until I could no longer see the shore and it was peaceful. I talked to God and I know he heard me. However he did not let me die then. The next day I was very curious and wondered if I had really done it, I mean fucked her. It was the first time and I wasn't even sure that I had!

First Living Room Window

The first true erotic opportunity did come a little later. I liked to think it happened when I was thirteen and she thirty-four. My awkward, over-thin, gangling puppy-frame at that age would have floundered on hers, ripe, rich, superb at the exact apex of her sexual force, happy, amused, touched, to initiate this child-man who had just shot up to his full adult height.

It happened easily enough, in the stateroom of that trans-Atlantic ocean liner on which I was traveling with my parents and little sister. I was starting on the sex hunt, but knew nothing of love relations, an innocent. My mother (and father? I don't know really, as if his presence were irrelevant: kind-natured, sentimental, obsessively concerned for her health—she outlived him by three decades—always apprehensive, utterly vulnerable, and no match at all for her. As she once told me, "You know, *mon petit*, in couples, one of the two is always dominant." In the last years of their life together, she had relegated him to the farthest corner of their gloomy mansion in Brussels, so that he not interfere in our obsessive relationship) and my sister and I were always on a ship heading in one direction or the other across the Atlantic. My mother was no doubt indulgently aware of my erotic ardors. For I had become interested in an older woman (older?! was she thirty? or thirty-four? what did I know!) on shipboard, and early one evening a woman had invited me into her cabin in order to help me with my bow tie. There was a definite erotic aura, I remember being terribly nervous and excited.

 I was aware of the woman's perfume and her backless gown which gave an air of nakedness, and I stood very close to her so that she could readjust my tie and perform the complicated loops and knots, her breasts (I could tell the outline of her nipples!) just grazing the jacket lapels of my first tuxedo as she leaned forward a little, my erection growing embarrassingly evident. If she had touched me down there, quite accidentally, I would have ejaculated immediately. But nothing happened at that time, I must have blurted some excuse and hurried out to conceal the cause of my extreme embarrassment, which no doubt would have offended her mortally. No, it could have been much later, after dinner at the captain's table, after the movie, after the evening bingo games, when they had all gone to bed. I sneaked out of the cabin which I shared with my sister (my parents so ignored my burgeoning sexuality that they still put us in the same cabin!) with my shoes in my hands, and putting my jacket on again but not the bow tie, hurried back to her cabin, and waited for minutes outside the door, not daring to breathe, listening for any evidence of her presence inside. Finally I tapped very lightly, shocked at my own boldness, and heard her voice call out. I couldn't move until the door opened a crack and she stood there, looking surprisingly small without her heels on, wearing a nightgown that revealed the deep cleavage of her breasts. She opened the door wider and pulled me in; I was shaken by the brusqueness of her gesture, and inside the cabin I just stared down at her as she stood revealingly, her body outlined in the filmy gown. Then she took both my hands and placed them on her breasts.

Ah, if it had happened that way, then perhaps I would not have been seduced by my mother as I was a few years later, because I would already have been initiated into the erotic delights of a lover. No doubt that is why she intervened when she did, having become aware of my so far ineffectual ardors. Alerted to the impending peril (oh my God why couldn't they have let things be?), she called me to her cabin in order to warn me about the perils of sex. Imagine, she told me, what happened to me the other day. "I tell you this, my sweet darling, because I want you to be aware of the dangers of sex. I had fallen into deep sleep on my bunk (probably had a glass too many at the captain's table yesterday evening, we were often invited, for my charms I believe, ha ha, she trilled), and abruptly I awoke with a strange feeling. I found the steward, who had apparently let himself into my cabin and had lifted my gown, unless it had fallen open during my drunken sleep, and he was busily lapping—she didn't say 'cunt' of course but her circumlocution was far more evocative—between my thighs. Of course I protested furiously and drove him from the room. So you see how careful one must be."

Why is it that I felt more than moral admonition in this graphic description, something of a connotation of rivalry? Of course it effectively ended my pending initiation by the other woman . . .

Second Living Room Window

My precocious intimations of maternal love were confirmed on the day when we drove off together on my holiday from college. Dad was away. It was glorious in her ancient convertible Chevy, the top down and the dark branches flashing above, her hair whipping about my arm behind her head, and for the first time I saw the strand of white hair coiled around her ear. I wish to describe this episode in its essence for it enfolds my entire life, but there are such distractions. Simply: I knew with an anxious thrill that I was violently, romantically in love with my mother. Her thigh pressed against mine in excited complicity, and I crooked my arm and fondled the nape of her neck, careful not to touch those curls, and she shot a curious and loving look at me as she drove with one-handed abandon, and I whispered to myself: see what's under her panties. She touched me between the thighs with proprietary interest, my, what have we here? she grinned. I laughed silently, nervously, and groped under her summery, gypsy dress: she had no panties. The soft little mound was damp. I inserted a finger clumsily, religiously, where

I could. And breathed deeply. I lay back, my head resting on the seat top, and watched the mountainous clouds streaming above. Lost in contemplation, I'd hardly noticed that she had unzipped my fly and was caressing the tumescent member with greedy solicitude. The moment soon came however when I did notice and then I cried out, Mummy!—immediately ashamed of the childish expression. She looked on absently, still rolling it, limp and moist, between her fingers. Darling, she said, you have to try to understand that your father and I . . . a distant look came into her eyes, violet with melancholy. I put it back in my pants and cried "look out!"—for the Chevy had drifted across the double line, and she jerked it back with a shuddering wrench of the frame and we bounced in our seats. I want to write something very pure and raw, about this grand love affair; it should be possible to tell the truth about what happened and how filial and erotic sentiments grew entwined and inextricable until they infested my innermost organs. Yes, I remember that drive and the unexpected cold in my heart and the insinuations in my ear and the pressure of her fingers on my organ. And I kissed her softly on the lips, she closed her eyes for seconds as we streaked down the middle of the two-way road at sixty-five miles an hour, Wheeeee! she cried as we hurtled on, and, Shut your eyes! I was the first to open my eyes and pulled desperately at the steering wheel, I was a hopeless driver. She snapped back and took the vehicle calmly in hand as I trembled. "Little man," she said, "don't be afraid. I'll nurture you, I'll teach you to wipe your little penis and to wash your hands." Motherly love. Ablutions. Soaked in it, awash in an ocean of love. Drowning in it. It was always tender, beautiful sex. Romantic sex. Not the dirty kind. That was for little boys playing alone with themselves. I squinted up into my mother's eyes, crafty. "Will you wear your black panties tonight," I asked in a low voice, "the ones with an open crotch?" "Oh, you're disgusting," she said, pouting, "you love the panties, not me." I squirmed, wishing my coccyx would fall off. I want to tell you in a simple and direct way how I fell in love with my mother and married her and lived happily ever after, being brought up by her—by that vaginal sea; the longing to stay beside it forever; the placental source, the viscous fluids. To leave it seems like death.

Third Living Room Window

So now comes the question of reality. And oddly, it was precisely at the point when I seduced and was seduced by her at the age of sixteen that I no longer could distinguish clearly between mother and lover. Yes, she did give birth to me. And yes, she was my lover. And now, a few years after the prior, fictitious, and perhaps preferable event, at the age of thirty-seven she was in her fullest bloom sensually and physically, keyed to the most exquisite pitch of her womanhood. At least this was my observation, I who after all had observed her—no, studied her—with such an intoxication of possession at various stages of her growth. For example, although most men might have judged her to be more perfectly desirable at the age of twenty-five, I (and I wasn't a man then) detected some shade of femaleness missing, a shadow on her bloom. "Glamorous" she certainly was, but some disillusionment had clouded and sharpened her features, no doubt my father's doing, which at age thirty-seven (and long divorced) had cleared away again and left her with the sweetness of the seventeen-year-old girl's face. So that you can imagine I was entranced by this net of recalls and correspondences. I say "net" because by now it was cast irrevocably. I first saw her in the carnal sense as a deliciously carnivorous female. She was dressed in black and leopard. When I asked her to dance that same evening she pulled in closely and sank down from tiptoe with her breasts pressed against me, so that these pulled upwards rolling on my chest, and I was hooked, transpierced, as surely as if she had sunk claws into my ribs instead. Oh I played the mature man, but at sixteen I was the child and she the mother-woman, taking what she wanted, what was hers. And I wanted to be taken, oh I wanted it. In the middle of that dancing throng only she existed as the old refrain goes, I was gobbled up in a trice, a mere morsel. When we "went to bed" later that night, that place of delectable execution—I was quaking with fear and desire, and she drew me to herself, I was wet, I was shuddering, she sucked me inside herself, her mouth, her body-mouth, her womb, her womb-tongue, the sweet teeth chewing me, eating me up, I screamed, I humped and I jumped in joy, the thick fluid spraying in the air, splashing her breasts, running in little rivulets over her tummy.

I don't even remember if we actually had intercourse that first time because she was in such control of the entire business. I was not doing it, it was being done to me. So this was reality! The sweet swell of her belly, the furry caress of her groin, the lapping of her tongue! It was in this instant that I knew I was not just a spectacle in the window. When I was rooted deep in her vulva, a root fed from her breeding miasma, tiny electrical impulses crackled at my nethermost tip and shuddered up along the root stock to explode in my groin and to charge the spine and the nerve constellations of my entire form: now I am this blind pulsation. Ephemerally. If I could remain in this charged state I would not have to see myself again through the glass. Glance very quickly before the flicker of recognition on the other side. But the spasm comes and I am discharged. If this is reality, why is it so painful now? My lover! Surely she is my lover! But the womb-source. I slid out of that womb, covered with primeval slime. I have returned to the womb, through the shattering glass and into the abyss. I look into my mother's eyes now. Isn't this the first time I have looked into her eyes? A moment ago I was selfless, fearless, hopeless, meaningless, heartless, thoughtless. Now I am malleable clay. She looks at me with such tenderness that I am lost. Mother, Mother, I suck at your nipples with infantile urgency. But their milk only makes me weaker. Mewing and puking. I desired you, I fucked you, my whore.

Fourth Living Room Window

From the very beginning of our romance, she had the gestures of tenderness or even a lover's greed. That day when I arrived at her apartment after having taken the train down from school in Cambridge, I was hardly inside the door when she fell on her knees before me, oh God the emotions were tearing at my throat, at last wholly her prey, but I couldn't even groan, and she feverishly unstrapped my belt and tore my zipper open and as I lay back against the wall, almost fainting, she devoured my genitals. This act of devouring, this taking possession, I see now as the passion of my mother, this flesh my flesh . . . And I, and I—afterwards, lying on the carpet with her before the roaring fireplace, I made the most tentative of gestures and discovered with a kind of religious awe the silk of her thighs and the startling penetrable fur of her mound. This was the discovery by a child of its mother's other being, furtively, astonished. However deep our shared sensuality, there was always a forbidden zone, a perimeter not so much physical as psychic, which neither she nor I could—or would—cross. I think our sexual passion, in those days, was not hindered by this ambiguity but doubled; as I guessed, beyond the tenderness of the lover's yielding thighs, at the compassion and the complicity of a mother.

First Dining Room Window

My mother had me when she was twenty-one, an alluring age. This age difference never bothered either one of us, in fact it seemed perfectly natural since we were mother and son, and if anything the intensity of our being lovers at first erased any difference. This was so true that I was always surprised when somebody, in a perfectly natural tone, asked, "Is she your mother?" or "Are you her son?" and at first I would answer with irritation, if not defiance, "No, she's my lover," because it seemed to me that they were deliberately ignoring what was obvious. I would glance at my interlocutor with suspicion, then realize there was nothing surreptitious, nothing insulting intended. Sometimes my mother would ask me what so and so had said in her absence, and I would invent something, not wishing to embarrass her with the person's observation of our age difference. I was so disturbed by these innocent queries that I would muse over the tone I would adopt on the next occasion, and what I could retort with: something with a slight sneer; or I considered answering with the truth, "Yes she is, we're lovers," but could never quite bring myself to it. As the years went by however, I became resigned to such questions, recognizing their innocence, and would answer, "Yes, she is my mother," or "Yes, I am her son," and was instantly moved by a peculiar tenderness on admitting it. Of course this caused some complications when she returned, I would have to avoid the kiss on the lips for instance or I would hold her in a less conjugal manner, or try to cover up some remark the other person might make in consequence, such as, "It's striking how alike you look," or "It's charming to see how he attends to you." Later however there was a further variation in my response: after having admitted that yes, she was my mother, to act normally with her, as my lover, aware of a curious erotic excitement as I watched for the troubled flicker of doubt in the other person's eyes. The emotional gap between our ages never shifted. When I was much younger and sometimes tried to imagine the future, I thought that with my own increased years I would begin to catch up with her, until we would finally coincide in old age. Sometimes I longed for that moment, to age toward her, so that we could be a normal couple. Instead an emotional geometry of time kept us locked into the same age differential, the fixed angle that held us apart never shifting in its psychic quantity. Only the quality of the relation changed. For example if at an earlier age I was the callow youth and she the seductress, later I became the mature male and she the ageing beauty. I felt it as an injustice that we could never come together in a symmetrical and reciprocal moment.

At the same time, as I felt in my bones this unyielding hardness of time, I became obsessed with possessing her at every moment of her life, including those years before I could remember her, or even before

I was born. I pored over her old photographs and questioned her closely about those years and tried to capture exactly the tone or savor of the time. She was a gifted storyteller of her own past, capable of inhabiting a particular moment with the same intimacy of emotion as if she were, for example, seventeen again, with no distance of reflection, no irony, no doubt, no abrasion of time and experience. Except for the first years of passion, during which I felt a dread of her past, as if it should not have existed, as it put a wedge between her and me, for many years after I experienced the opposite emotion, a passion to know her as intimately as possible at every moment in the past, to be able to love her when she was twenty-six or twenty-seven, arrogant, dominantly beautiful, supremely egotistic and worshipped by any male approaching her; or at the age of sixteen or seventeen, as she was just coming to an awareness of the womanhood awakening within her, of wounded delicacy, observing the arcs of motion of bodies in space, full of an undefined yearning and talking to the moon, romantically suicidal, lonely in her narcissistic self-reflection, yet as sure of her effect on the other sex as that of the radiant sun on her tropical land.

There was one photograph of my mother at that age that is fixed indelibly in my heart: her mother is seated on a chair in the garden of her house with a proud, possessive manner, while she sits on the arm of the chair, and glances down and to the side with the purity of a virgin from a fifteenth-century Flemish painting, away from the photographer, a sweetness apparent in the softness of her cheek and her inclined brow that steal my breath away. In that moment I want to step forward and put my life at her feet but some shadow arrests me. Or at the age of twelve, sexuality just burgeoning in her body, an awkward, plump age, a fullness of life bursting within her, a delightful, impish comrade, playmate, little sister. But already a girl older men look at knowingly and nod their head over, envious of the future. Or at the age of six or seven, saucy, irrepressible, possessed of the same assurance she would recover again in her twenties and thirties, with the shining gaze of a cat, a child so beautiful and unnervingly direct that adults would be afraid of her if they were not so charmed. With this child I know what it is to be an adulatory father. I step forward to collect her into my arms, but she breaks away, elusive and explosive always, her laughter sparkling in my mind. I have lived my life with my mother dreaming of what it would be like to be her father—and her lover.

Second Dining Room Window

My dual sex dreams: one time I was lying in bed with my mother and another man. It seemed that I was a (female?) prostitute paid to have sex with him. He undressed, displaying shaved pudenda. I realized it was an artificial vagina. I became immediately disgusted and rang room service for a drink, signifying that I am not accepting the transaction. What was my mother's attitude all the while? Observant?

Another time I was unfaithful to my mother; I was definitely a woman and I had made a date with a handsome man at a dinner party. Then I realized I had been very stupid, since I already had a rendez-vous with Mother at the same party. Although I had a clear-cut memory of being a woman, she was not a man, or perhaps was something between a man and a woman. All this is dubious, but there was no doubt that the other man (my father?) was her rival for my affections. At the dinner party, a very large gathering, scores of people in several rooms, I wandered about looking for my date. Then I understood he had decided not to come, apparently because he had realized there were complications—much to my disappointment (but also relief, because of Mother's imminent arrival). Now she appeared at the top of the staircase, brandishing several of my agendas, open. As if in a close-up I saw she had discovered the pages in which I had reported on my infidelities and of the waves of rage and shame which overcame me on all those past occasions when she had called me to confession of my thoughts and temptations, recorded in those scribbled and often blacked-out notes, which she triumphantly pointed at now. It was clear that my infidelity had been found out.

Later she actually did tell me that the day after each of our screaming matches she would read what I had written down immediately afterwards in my notebook in frustrated exhaustion and, incredulous at my viciousness and spite, would then call me to her room in order to question me again, but of course without alluding to the fact that she had been reading those notes, in order to preserve this valuable access to my secret mind . . . The new line of questioning would produce fresh outrage in me, a new entry in my notebook, and so on. This she had been doing for years, she told me, and my realization of the absurdly gratuitous, self-generating nature of our discord was curiously liberating, almost unbelievably comic and pitiful . . .

Third Dining Room Window

From my agenda

May 21st: For this occasion of my punishment, Mother dressed severely and wore the shadow of a moustache; she appeared of uncertain age. She required that I either wear a clinical gown or be naked while she interviewed me. Her preference was clearly the former, mine the latter with my penchant for exhibitionism. I could easily imagine her as an officer in a Death Camp interested in behavioral experiments with inmates of both sexes. After my interview, during which she asked me why I hated women (a hypothesis I had never entertained in all my introspections), she left me with the list of preferences I had drawn up for the session. While she was gone I was able to examine at leisure the volumes in her bookcases—the classics of revolutionary feminism and a large variety of exotic cookbooks. Soon the two girls she had selected for my needs appeared, both dressed in the minimal garter belt and half-bra uniform, and proceeded to cross-dress me in mirrored gear—tight panties and stretched garters— and then arranged me on the specially constructed bed where they tied my arms down to the lateral bars and legs upward and apart, pulled back toward the chest, to the overhead bars, rear in the air, and proceeded to follow instructions scrupulously, inserting the implement effectively and more painfully in reality than I had expected (fantasies are always painless). After the session I met with Mother again and expressed my appreciation in the customary monetary terms.

Mother's First Bedroom Window

Why did I have to suffer like this if she was my mother? Shouldn't she have been understanding, all-suffering? Instead I suffer, I scream in agony! See my agenda:

Nov. 18: Mother and I have been bloodying one another for more than three weeks now. This morning she appeared at my bed (separate beds) at 5 A.M. and started in. We have not moved an inch. I feel half-destroyed and no doubt she as well. I believe her reasoning is insane, but she is convinced there is some enigma which explains my conduct, and perhaps she (after all) is right. We have come to our end. Any subject raised in this spiral of recriminations, such was my notorious Confession (a madman's!) almost twenty years ago (that was a mistake!), awaken the same rage and passion now as it did then. The insoluble irritant is this: not the enigma which she seeks to uncover through these endless cross-examinations—by now no secret is left!—but the ever-present catalogue of my faults and offences which she untiringly reviews, and which no repentance or reform on my part (if I still so desired) could ever efface, and which is susceptible of being called up at any and every occasion in the future. I know this as surely as I know my feces, or my death.

Mother's Second Bedroom Window

I ask you again, why should I have suffered like this if she were my mother? But isn't every man the son of his lover at some point? And what is the accurate point then, the sensitive moment at which distortion begins? It is when she has pity on you, or when you have pity on her, the knot of tenderness. That is the point at which the blood begins to ooze. Hello my darling, hello. My mummy, I kiss your sweet lips, I am dying in your embrace. I am your child and your fucker. I enter your sweet cunt and I am not sure that I will ever come out again, perhaps I will drown inside this infinite, murky, bitter sea. I have tasted your liquors, they intoxicate and embitter, poison me. Although your poison tasted sweet! Ah my woman, my mother, I have drunk at your obscene chalice, I have drunk to the dregs. My lips are dark with your blood. And still you won't forgive me? I shall drink more in order that I may be entirely intoxicated, for sobriety is not conducive to romantic relations.

Mother's Bathroom Window

Confession, however, elicits lies. It might seem the opposite at first blush, but lies and deception flow inexorably out of confession. Because full, luxurious, soul-scraping confession, which is the sort one makes to one's mother (not one's lover!—only the mother exercises such ineluctable authority) implies total transparency. No one can live in a window constantly, only during this moment of confession. And even then. Yes, consider the case of some who do live in a window, such as the whores of Amsterdam and Brussels and a few other European cities, and whom I once frequented assiduously. The window conceals more than it actually reveals. Unlike the street-corner prostitute, who stands in for one's mother or lover, and whose body, her proximity, her perfume, her solid dimensions, are squarely on display in the flesh, and even available on request to the probing touch, the window-display "dummy"-prostitute inhabits a mysterious inner space and cannot be touched, since what the window conceals in actuality is that there is no mystery. Its transparency reveals whatever she wishes regarding her role and her props but no more. And so in the complete, denuding, "religious" confession one reveals only in order to conceal the essential. And this essential concealed truth is doubtless the reason why the confession quickly generates an unceasing flow of new lies and deceptions in order to cover the nakedness nearly uncovered, to reconstruct the character in question: one's own—in appearance. So my new lies corresponded to the triviality of my transgressions. These were innumerable: the glance of a passing girl, the erotic aura of momentarily revealed panties from the bottom of a staircase, the frottage of the street crowd, onanistic experimentation, Mother's lingerie, all so many childish misdeeds that disappointed, no, enraged Mother because they revealed the child behind the man she had constructed around the child like a pasteboard figure, and which she needed in order to render decent or palatable the relationship which she had entertained with her own child. And so I engaged in a hasty, collaborative, reconstructive effort following my conscientious confession. But it must not be thought the Confession was the matter of a moment, a transient lucidity. No, it was the work of weeks, of months, it might even be said of the rest of our lives together. The Confession was a joint undertaking, the collaboration of interrogator and criminal, or of tormentor and victim. In my first naïve élan I thought to deliver my soul of all its guilty offenses and lay them at the feet of my mother, and then have done with it. Instead we went through an endless, painful work of dissection, unpeeling one bloody strand from the other, extracting from a dark core an even darker core. The refinement, the delicate shades of defining and separating out the parts of transgression over the years, were in their manner exquisite, if equally painful for both of us. I remember after one of the first sessions that I drank myself into a stupor in order to escape her. Instead, as I lay sick, vomiting, sweating, the tears streaming down my face, she screamed and shook me, asking the same questions over and over again, slapping me as though she wanted to break some shell. Finally, as if in a dream, something did seem to break, and as I wept she cradled me like a child. I only understood much later that what had shattered was my sense of self. Of course as the years went by it became impossible to discover new tones, new indices, in the recital of sins, and so as the "child's" inventiveness flagged but the mother's cross-examination never did, it took on a dull sameness, a repetitiousness which was even more exhausting than the previous moral research, not merely the recital but the relations it fixed between us; she the accuser, I the defendant, I the aggressor, she the wounded, and I the child, she the mother: rigid ratios, a constellation we are set in. It wasn't bitterness that drove this wheel around, but frustrated love.

Pantry Window

Airless, this pantry. I don't think it really has a window, but of course it must have, for here I am in full sight. In this house what is bizarre is that one never looks out of the windows to the outside world but only inwards . . . I am of the opinion that we—my mother and I—only looked inwards as well, even though we were inside. When you think about it, it is hardly surprising that this environment should be suffocating, because the house seems only to have windows, which in normal circumstances would suggest air, light, openness, but not in here, because there is no door! I don't really like this artificial ambience, but it's important to realize—we never did realize it—that our language forms our house; more, that it really is our house. I needed fresh air! My mother, in the course of one of our games of accusation and self-denunciation, dared me to leave her if that was what I wanted, and suddenly I made for the door, but I had barely placed my hand on the knob when she caught me again, not physically, but reeling me back on a fine but unbreakable line of emotional blackmail. "There is no door there," she said. "Mother," I said, "this is the first time you have actually spoken to me of a door. Why isn't there a door?" "Because you can't go out." In effect she was right, although awfully circular: a door supposes that one can actually go in or out. The mere reference to a door was enough to get me thinking about it. I used to practice when she wasn't there, just walking out the door—actually packing a bag and walking out. When I finally did leave my mother—even now it sticks like a knife in my throat—she fell to the ground holding onto my legs, the mascara running in rivulets down her face, begging me not to leave her. She thought I never could.

First Window of the Basement Room

Of course, the trouble with my relationship with her was that I was after all passionately in love—at first. Do you know what most pained me after I left her? I always thought it was unhappiness for her, worry over her, the need to protect her, but I think I've got at something more fundamental: that nobody would ever love me as she had. I arrived at this conclusion in a curious and telling way. I asked myself: if I were impaired sexually (an odd question, this imaginary self-castration), who—of any potential female candidates—would love me the most? The answer was obvious, my mother. My lover would not put up with it, or only if there were some sort of bargain, some quid pro quo involving third parties (after all, wouldn't that be my own position? Lovers are equals and pitiless). But my mother . . . she would do anything! But why precisely this condition of sexlessness? In the basement of our house I practiced a recurring fantasy. I would tie myself up naked, with only her panties or garter-belt on, and I did so in a precarious position, leaving the last of the sliding knots, a sort of noose, about one wrist, just within reach. It could quite easily slip out of my reach, and I would find myself then in the inextricable position of a bound, cross-dressed clown (or victim?), helpless to free myself, with flagrant evidence of my moral degradation. Why this desire to disappoint or shock my mother? I knew her reaction would be disgust and wry derision. Was this my real desire, to be mocked? or insulted? Maybe. There was the time I had Mother tie me, or rather handcuff me, to an attachment in the ceiling, naked of course, except for a pair of her panties or camisole. She circled around me, whipping me on the posterior and elsewhere—under cover of the lingerie, which however afforded little protection. Part of the bargain was that she insult me and even spit on my lower body. She didn't need to touch me. The climax of course was the sudden wetting of the garment.

Second Window of the Basement Room

Notwithstanding the above, I was always extremely courtly with her. When we went out, on ever-rarer occasions, I would escort her—in other words, we would not really walk together like a normal couple, but I would be her knight errant. I was aware, in myself, of a certain stiffness, a formality, in my attitude of protecting her against a hostile world. What hostility? There is no mockery in this, it was evident that she had a vulnerability, and a majesty, that should not be touched by the world, *ningun roce* in her tongue, she had to be spared frictional contact. Of course it was also a matter of self-protection. It is curious how this stiff formality on my part was a kind of exo-skeleton. Of course! Because this was the persona she demanded. For my sex-mother was savagely jealous. When I walked by her side I had to keep my eyes straight ahead, as if I wore blinkers. And of course the more rigidly I trained my vision, the more lasciviously and viscously my eyes were tugged by the passing women. If we happened to pass an attractive woman, I looked in the opposite direction with a slight air of ennui, not too marked of course because she could catch the slightest nuance, and yet my head was being tugged backwards as if by an erotic elastic. Not that I didn't find my mother and lover beautiful: sometimes I would glance at her and it was if a radiance broke through her skin, as if she were more beautiful than any immediate physical perception, and my soul was delighted with her—but my body continued to act quite independently.

There was one absurd incident in our house (well, my mother's house): she had recently hired a new woman to clean, a brutish type right out of one of Goya's dark paintings (my mother was so fair and blue-eyed she was almost diaphanous), and once when she was laboring with a huge bucket of soapy water I obligingly carried it to the next spot in one of those quixotic, meaningless gestures of courtliness which I have with women, any woman. She expressed excessive gratitude and my mother glowered at me with such rage that I quickly put it down again. Afterwards she screamed at me with contempt for making a fool of myself and of her in front of another woman. That was, she raged, exactly what the cleaning woman wanted. This incident is one of many which continued to feed our violent clashes for the next twenty-one years.

Later that afternoon, from a discrete vantage point, I happened to observe the cleaning woman as she soaped the floor on all fours with her rump toward me, while the vigorous movements she made caused her oversized breasts to swing heavily. She stopped for a few minutes to rest without changing position, while keeping a watchful eye on the kitchen door which lay beyond and ahead of both of us, no doubt in case her mistress, my mother (who thrived on the servant-mistress relationship with its subtle mix of feminine confidences and browbeating), should emerge, and her relaxed rump sloped upwards in that position, and her dress was pulled just above a pantiless groin and thus a large and feral pubic mound was exposed. I stared in disgust and fascination for at least a full minute, then quickly retreated to safety, breathless and trembling, my member viscid. So after all, "a posterior(i)", Mother's jealous rage was justified. But it was often like this. It seemed that her jealousy, which most often, at least at first, lacked any real object, would create one out of sheer concentration.

Kitchen Window

I often thought (or wanted to think?) that it was my mother's early bursts of jealous rage that pushed me into my first infidelities. This is not what I want to speak of now however, but of their curious and devastating effect: that as I grew progressively apart from her in sexual desire, my emotions became more and more tender and filial to the point of unbearable sorrow and pain with the presentiment of my pending betrayal and abandonment. A ratio seemed to operate between these sentiments, and it was an unexpected, absurd and yet predictable conclusion that when finally all erotic bonds were severed between us, at that moment the agony of filial loss and want was swollen out of all former proportion. It was as if now the sweet, half-desired but half-dreaded ambiguity of erotic union with the mother had suddenly given way to a purer longing for the motherly comforts. Oddly, then, my new forbidden lusts were more than matched by a paroxysm of filial yearning. Once, after all sexual bonds between us had been severed, she proposed to wear new, exotic lingerie for me. I was filled with disgust and pity, and felt remorse at my own reaction. She had become the original mother again for me, before "the fall." The final reversal of relations took place with geometrical exactness: at the very moment I reached the age at which my mother had me, I had my daughter.

Window of the Boiler Room

The night before mother's funeral I fucked a prostitute. I don't remember anything about the prostitute. I wanted to be united with *her* in death. A cloying taste. Did the prostitute guess she was standing in for death? Or lying down . . . or on top. But it was very difficult to have any intimacy with her body, especially since she had herself cremated. Little fiery, then black specks. Only that smell remains, sickeningly sweet. Oh, where is your body?

Part II

Entrance Hall Door

But why the affair with my daughter just now? Because the isosceles triangle, in which the difference between her age and mine exactly equaled the difference between my mother's and mine when we first began to "live" together, had been formed. Each side of the triangle represented a corresponding segment of our lives: my childhood and adolescent life as my mother's sexual plaything; my adult life and "marriage" to my mother; my daughter's coming of age. The fixity of the triangle appeared to represent a hieratic, ineluctable succession—both frightening and intoxicating. What I didn't immediately realize when I drew into my daughter's wake was that our love affair would have to be torn out of the integument I shared with Mother, and for all the joy that the union with my daughter would yield, to that exact degree the pain of separation from my mother would be inflicted. This was inscribed in the invariability of our triangular relationship. I felt the pain intimately as if living tissue was being torn out of my chest and belly, and I tried to suppress my groans at night so that my daughter wouldn't hear.

The night of our first coupling was on the occasion of a professional commitment—our camaraderie was entirely new and intoxicating to me, even her manner of helping me was sweetly filial and alluring—a reversal of what I had experienced with my mother, whom I had always helped—in the filial role. I did not realize at the time that the triangle of reversals and inverse ratios would affect all our relations, and when we finally went to the bedroom together, it seemed so natural and inevitable to me to unbutton her blouse and pull off her pants so that she lay naked before me, and to bury my face in her sweet furry triangle as years before my own mother had devoured my cock. Was this an act of homage? The first two or three times we fucked, the ecstasy of orgasm was so intense that it felt as though the back of my head was being torn off, until she taught me to release the contractions of pain that ran up my spine to the base of my neck during the act. But I know in retrospect that what was being wrenched from my mind was the residue, the memory of my erotic love for the mother. It also strikes me that I have never actually described an act of sexual intercourse with the latter. And this is only natural, because although she was a passionate woman, her passions were absorbed in the emotion of love, and the act of fucking, which for my daughter was pure pleasure, was only incidental for my mother, incidental to the bond between us. So that my daughter was the interior door for me, not an object of endless speculation but the principle way into a woman.

The Entrance Toilet Door

From the very beginning, getting to know my sweet daughter carnally, I delighted in buying her different styles of lingerie; for example, a white virginal camisole in which her small breasts and large dark nipples swung loosely, matched with tiny bikini panties through whose fretted lace-work in sharp contrast the dark furrow of her pubic hair outlined the little mound, and behind, the connecting silky strip rolled between her firm cheeks. Or the loose black panties which, a campy lingerie salesman salaciously lisped to me, were known as witch's britches and which floated about her hips with filmy tactility. This least revealing of lingerie was the most exciting, because, theatrically, it only suggested, or let one divine, what secret life lay within. Then there were the whorish (from a porno shop in the much frequented "rue de la Gaité" in Paris) red crotchless panties with garter belt and the open-nippled bra, which she wore just once in the up-scale "hôtel de passe," the by-the-hour hotel of Les Camelias with its useful mirrors. She laughed in disbelief but wore them nonetheless in the bedroom scene I proposed to her. And countless other variations: the narrow-crotch panties, the thong panties where the subtle cord disappeared completely between the posterior cheeks. These were her favorite, she wore them all the time, and I suspected she derived some unavowed pleasure from them. My girl loved these interior dressing-scenes as much as I did, and would parade with a charming mix of shyness and mockery in garter-belt and stockings minus panties for example. For us both it was a little theatre of the erotic in which the diverse lingerie projected the roles of ingenue, whore, mistress, innocent, and sometimes the most demure of chiffon camisoles became the most provocative because of the childish aura they leant her. These articles of female dress were part-costume, part-prop, and part-stage machinery, with their delicate straps and cords, their ambiguity of veiling and revealing, and their various stage functions. One of the more delectable schemes she invented for my delight was her insistence that I take her roughly with panties still on—just twisting them out of the way or pulling the crotch outward so tightly that the panties dug between the cheeks of her ass.

Because I have opened the door to the toilet, it seems an apt place to consider a peculiar, hitherto unknown pleasure I took with my delicious girl: peeing. Unthinkable with my beloved mother! She and I both had an uninfringeable taboo regarding such matters; we even took pains to keep our excretions secret from one another. I must admit that to hear my mother peeing would disgust me and put me off the idea of sex altogether. In some curious way it was as if—the sexual prohibition having been clearly flouted—the negative charge had shifted to the excretory functions. In an odd reversal, as soon as I began to have sexual relations with my girl, I wanted to know the feeling of her *piss* on my body. I asked her to squat over me in the bath and piss on my stomach and on my groin. How can I explain that exquisite percolation? The delicate stream at first trickled shyly between my thighs, but then grew bolder, and her hot stream jetted into my groin and against my balls. It was her self-abandon—and her confidence—that delighted me, her desire to give me pleasure. She laughed out loud when she saw my reaction and the pleasure I took for myself, and she laughed as well at her own daring and her mock offense against the prostrate father. And I saw in her widened pink crack above and in the transparent sparkling plume a gift of herself, a generosity which was more than that of a woman giving herself to a man. It took me a little longer to dare to piss on her, but when I did the first time—it was in the shower as we bathed together—and she bent down in front of me, her head close to the floor, in order to enjoy the sensation of the hot water cascading along her back—the sight of the sweet curve of her ass and the childishness of her posture were so bewitching that, after some intense but fruitless straining, and then an attempt to overcome my inhibition by mental detachment from the spectacle of her innocent body, I began to piss on her back, my slight arc blending with the shower spray. I told her what I was doing, and she pretended to be indignant, without moving, and then laughed with fun and pushed her ass up higher in the direction of my stream, and it splattered on her ass and thighs. My legs trembled violently as I pissed on her lithe young back, but the pleasure again was more than physical: it was a fullness of emotion at her readiness to accept this act, and at the same time a sweetness in the intimacy of polluting my baby. Later her back door would open into a more interior dimension of the pleasure in her soiling.

Father's Bedroom Door

And what of the face we turned to the public? Her jet-black hair which sloped as smooth as shantung silk against my hand, and the sole silver hair I could find in it? I'd once had the same, almost Chinese-black hair and still did here and there spilling out below the silver. From the first it enchanted me to capture the residue of the child, the girl, in her, and to think of her deliberately as my little girl. Yet she was never childish with me, although she sometimes played the child—we were comrades, pals. She liked to drive, and so I often left the driving to her—she was a better driver than me anyway, even virile and aggressive in this activity as in our sexual relations. After gently caressing me while driving, she loved to extract my rigid penis from my pants and masturbate me, keeping full control of me and of the wheel, teasing me that she was going to stop, glancing at me in my state of helpless excitement, and laughing with pleasure when I overflowed. But when I fucked her, she would cling to me and ask in a childish plaintive voice, over and over, why I was doing this to her. I reassured her that I was only doing something that was good for my little girl, and that it gave her Daddy so much pleasure. I told her she was my baby whore, and she would protest weakly that she was not a whore at all, but my little girl. I used the crudest, most vulgar language because she craved it, describing exactly what I was doing with my cock and my finger or thumb while she melted with pleasure. I became furiously ardent, barely able to resist violent impulses like slapping or biting. When she was in that humor herself, she exercised no restraint whatsoever. When she played pussy cat she would crawl about the floor on all fours meowing, wearing only her panties. Then suddenly she would dash at me with a growling scream and bite me on the thighs and genitals and scratch me till I bled. I carried my bruises with amusement and half-concealed pride before my male friends. If anybody openly addressed her as my daughter—although that was still rare—I was charmed. The passion I felt for her was only inflamed by this perception through another's eye of the character of our relationship.

Any social life that I once shared with my mother had soon collapsed inwards, and from then on it was always determined by our interior life, limited to a few close friends who could be trusted to respect our special relationship. In fact any rare forays out of this narrow circle were fraught with a sense of peril, and so my attention was hardly ever turned outward toward others (and never toward the other sex. Although I was extremely alert I would still invariably trip into some disastrous pitfall—the occasions of sin which I was to pay for dearly in the persecutions of Mother. Of course as a consequence I felt myself drawn outward toward the other sex violently in elastic self-extrusion. After any such occasion of body-self exteriority I quickly snapped back into our mutually "transparent" household of emotion. Whereas with my girl, our attention was turned entirely outward. After all, we could go in and out of doors effortlessly, the Front Door was unlocked whenever we wished to use it. Being with her came to mean being with others. I openly appreciated the charms of any woman I met in her company, consequently the gravitational tension between us was minimal. As if there was a natural harmony in these mutual orbits instead of the anxiety to pull out of orbit that I had experienced with my mother, and which "mechanically" was countered by her with an equal and opposite inward-sucking tension. I had learned to deal with her suspicions with agility. Mutatis mutandis, it cost me real effort to learn to accept the same "social" availability on my daughter's part—a not small torment, the first time she went out with another man—platonically, or so I convinced myself. I did learn, and just like I might desire some other woman on occasion (although in reality this was not the case, I thought I ought to test my exclusive and overpowering passion for my girl), it no longer seemed so unlikely that my daughter might share the same desires as I once experienced when with my mother. In fact I had no desire to test anything at all, and to picture anybody else with her made my heart bleed.

Main Bathroom Door

With my daughter I was in a state of almost constant tumescence. It makes me wonder if "my mother seen through the bathroom window" might really have been my daughter? In any case, I wanted to fuck her all the time. And when I fucked her it was not by some circuitous route, pretending something else, as I had been obliged to do with my mother—I mean an act of romance, of romantic love abstracted from the physical, so that toward the end of our affair it had become so difficult to fuck without really fucking that it all dwindled to nothing. Although it had begun in passion with my mother, it became so overlaid with resentments and—precautions— exacerbated sensibilities and rigid patterns, that I had to go to the whores. But my girl, my sweet woman—she was more of a whore than any whore I had ever known! I didn't need to supply a romantic masquerade for her cunt. When I fucked her I thought of nothing else; this had never happened before. The fucking was complete in itself. Just purest pleasure. Early in our relationship as lovers, I almost did die in that warm vaginal sea I'd dreamed of in my boyhood. This incident followed several days of estrangement and agony over my "betrayal" of Mother, for which I blamed myself bitterly, because of the joy I was taking now with my daughter on the subtropical beaches of Bahia. I had been told there were treacherous currents but I thought I could make it anyway, as I swam across the choppy waters toward an island a mile off the shore. I talked to God on that trip. I drifted mentally and physically, happy in an anesthetized haze. Great tableaux of my life floated in the wash of the waves before my eyes. When my girl picked me up (she had set off to look for me in a boat with friends in some abrupt intuition of danger, and by miracle intercepted me), I was half roasted by the noonday sun. I would certainly have drifted to my death on that maternal sea had it not been for her.

❧

Since my girl loved to play at being violated, it was only a small step to "forcing" her. I took the most intense pleasure in tying her up, slipping nooses around her wrists and tying the rope to the sides of the bed, then tying her ankles apart as well. She didn't cooperate but resisted if not with all her strength, giggling hysterically, and protested angrily or pleaded with me. For my part, my legs trembled and my heart beat hard, but the sight of her helplessness was delectable—it corresponded exactly to the nature of my paternal feelings for her in an enhanced mode— moved by the childish pretense of vulnerability and troubled by her lascivious desire. I resisted her blandishments or fits of pique until I had her properly trussed up. Then with tender deliberation I would perform certain acts upon her, touching, exploring and finally penetrating her. While I did so she used a dozen registers to urge, beg, order, threaten, cajole and "speak sensibly" with me in order to get me to release her. She was not above biting hard or scratching. It often reached a point where I began to doubt that she was playing with me, wondering if she was seriously upset, and so would untie her, at which she would immediately burst out laughing, delighted at having fooled me, rubbing her chafed wrists. I would always promise myself that next time I would ignore her protests and "rape" her in earnest, but I could rarely get beyond the early stage of play, and whenever she succeeded in dispelling the suspension of belief that had allowed us to enter into the mock-rape, I would be defeated again. Why did I take such pleasure in these games? I think because the fragility and weakness she played at as my "little girl," which so moved me when we had sexual relations, was doubled when she was bound, willing/unwilling. Or, put the other way around, because the plaintiveness she provoked me with when I took her normally lead me to augment the erotic tension by binding her. Was it because I wanted to render her passive, an object of my desire? To do with her what was my pleasure? No. She easily defused that. By going limp. By becoming a "doll"—"One of those inflatable dolls, baby!" She just lapsed into inert flesh, and I could take no more pleasure. No, I think the reason was the enchantment of the erotic comedy we played—at which she always excelled.

Then there was the implement, the "toy" as she called it, and which she had carefully chosen. Sometimes when I had her tied up, I would "ply" her with it, and its insertion was not that violation I had experimented on myself (when Mother played the game of the prison warden), nor did it produce the grotesque image it had represented for me then and which was its synesthetic aim—on the contrary, with her it was charm, play, shyness and boldness mixed, utterly capricious and immodest, groaning with pleasure one moment and with pain at the next, begging me to withdraw it from a particularly sensitive spot and then begging me not to. For me this form of penetration was an amazing discovery of her as entirely separate from myself, almost a different species. She once told me I was like a small boy discovering sex for the first time. But why now, after all the women I had known before her? What she didn't realize is that she was the newness, her self-offering, at once offered and then withdrawn, spirited away. It was as if the world were very young again, to discover her with this fascination for her sex; it was as if the tedium of the last days (and nights!) with Mother had been washed aside.

Mother's Bathroom Door

Sometimes we played in the bathtub together: once, when we stayed at the empty family holiday home by the Lake of Geneva. The old house was alive—or should I say moribund?—with memories, because it was the place where, one night so many years ago, my mother had slammed the door on me, and I had left with nothing but the shirt on my back. I was distinctly aware of the ghosts of my mother and father, adding a slightly morbid flavor to our games. Facing each other reclining in the bathtub was a tight fit, and we had to interlace our legs. Her legs passed over my thighs and her feet were wedged under my arms. In such a position, ass pressed against ass, my legs disappeared under the water and under her body, and inevitably my cock assumed a vertical position and stuck up between her thighs, nestling against her pubic hair. She played with it crying, "Look, look, I've got a cock!" And with her small breasts and the cock stuck in her groin and her short-cropped hair, for a moment she might have been a pretty boy masturbating. It was near-hallucinatory: even though it was my member, it appeared to be hers, and she handled it as if it were indeed hers. For the first time in my life I felt a stir of homosexual excitement, as I watched her playfully pretend to be masturbating, but of course it was I who came. This was a peculiarly ambiguous occasion, and it only reinforced the identity I felt with her. Of course I also identified with my mother, but that was because she had absorbed me into her ego in an emotional osmosis. With my girl, the feeling was of a little sister and comrade—sometimes in her eyes I saw this—a sister, so intimate, so friendly, a sister I could fuck (every brother's dream)! We both had those hazel eyes that shift to green. After she had masturbated herself/me that evening, she turned around in the tub on her knees with her back to me and her head resting on her arms on the floor of the tub. Kneeling behind her I fucked her wildly, and she buried her face underwater and the bubbles rose up in effervescence. Her posture was at once child's play and an erotic provocation. Sometimes I felt as if our lovemaking were a corollary of my mother's and mine. Why shouldn't fucking be more playful, I used to ask my mother. As if I had a premonition of my daughter.

My Mother's Bedroom Door

I was surprised and fascinated by my girl's menstrual blood. Something which was never mentioned by my mother. In fact, I can only remember one occasion when the subject was raised early on in our relationship, and that was when I made some tasteless joke about her not needing Tampax. She flew into a rage, as if a sacred threshold had been violated, and I only realized why on reflection: because she went into menopause quite soon after our liaison, and considered any such reference a deadly insult to her womanhood. I was duly chagrined. To the contrary, my sweet girl bled quarts, and I enjoyed this womanly mystery-cycle (remember—I had only really known my mother as intimately until now) enormously. At high tide love-making wasn't possible, but otherwise, blood and all, I was invited in. A day or so after the flash flood, her invitations would grow quite pressing. Afterwards I would withdraw and gaze with a mixture of absurd pride and even more absurd horror at the stains on my member. I felt such intimacy with her that I needed to be anointed by every fluid of her body. Maybe this need for liquefaction was why, at that first love-making, I had pulled off her jeans and panties and buried my face in the labile goblet between her legs to drink.

Living Room Door

I realize that to the outsider, my relationship with my sweet girl might appear exclusively sexual or physical. And that would be a mistake. What appeared to be purely sexual was in reality, beneath the surface, intensely emotional, and, what may be more disconcerting to the prurient onlooker, spiritual. But I beg you to believe me when I say that while I fucked my girl I thought of nothing: not of fucking, not even of not thinking; my mind was focused uniquely on the physical penetration. There had been no other occasion of my life in which I was so single-minded. For those minutes the mental chatter had died down. I am reminded of the time we climbed a hilly path alongside a stream in southern Brazil, guided by a local boy, in order to find a little waterfall he knew of. When we found it we stripped and lay together in the stream with our heads under the chilly splash of the spring for a cleansing baptism, while he watched with curiosity. She in her spiritualist way hoped I would be cleansed of the tormenting demons of my guilty conscience at having abandoned my mother.

Dining Room Door

For example, the luxury of truthfulness. Unlike my relationship with my mother, when, after my earliest catastrophic attempts at truthfulness—I told her I was attracted to other women in the streets, or that I was excited by their proximity in the crush of the subway—I learned to guard my words and my eyes, even my thoughts (and even the most secret of these were less guarded than I thought: witness the notebooks in which I jotted down my intimate rages and frustrations), even the purloined affairs of my dreams (I could hardly tell her what I had been dreaming "last night" although she often was unduly curious and pressed me—was there some early-morning manifestation I had not concealed?). But to my girl I could say anything that passed through my head—and I did. This ability to be truthful and open was not an obligatory transparency (the obligation to be transparent) was both demanded and rendered impossible by my mother, because of the underlying threat: confession (mine), which for Mother was an obsession, was *non compos mentis* for my daughter and me, for we recognized each other's private spheres. Truthfulness was simply a further luxury, something to be savored, a delight of the spirit. It was an offering of the spirit, much like the offering of her body and the innocent lasciviousness of her gestures. A gift.

The knot of pity: of self-pity or of pity solicited from the other: this is another way of binding the hands and feet of one another, but not for sweet pleasure. It had become an elaborate game with my mother, but for my daughter it was a ridiculous—and damaging—game to be avoided like a disease. And worst of all, the competition of pity: who is most pitiable, most sick, most unsatisfied, most unrequited, and hence most deserving of pity! The problem was, of course, that if you were most to be pitied, then you had no energy to waste on pitying, and the other owed you his (it was never her) pity. The pity equation was ideally suited to our mother/son relationship. Even years after our separation, the memory of a sob or a groan from my mother would choke me with tears.

Basement Door

In bed I used to watch her face—more than just beauty it was the rapid flux of womanly emotions which touched my damaged heart, because if there was one sentiment that has dominated every other for me it was this sense of her womanliness. Though one might have expected this feeling also to characterize my relationship with my mother—since after all it was with her that I discovered sex—it did not. For her I had a filial tenderness which precluded her dimension as woman. Whereas I delighted in my daughter's capriciousness, the way in which her mouth and eyes wrinkled up when she cried, her sometimes arbitrary and often menstrual storms of temper, and when she leaned her face on her hand and gazed down at me in bed, and how the palm of her hand pulled one eye up into a slanted Chinese gaze, and her entirely novel and childlike wisdom, because they all appeared to me as little epiphanies of her womanhood. And it was all the more strange, since my mother was actually the more "feminine," with all the vulnerability of the "help me! provide me with anything I need, I am only a woman!" neurosis, whereas my girl had a virile side—initiative, enterprise, organization—and called forth my own feminine side, my "anima," which had never emerged under the Queen's reign, where my one role had been clearly defined (by her) as knight errant, as *caballero andante*. This role had been exhausting, since I could never relax and simply be myself, always having to play the role of the gentleman with his lady, with all the proper attributes and manners. Perhaps that's why I became so interested—personally interested—in her underclothes. I could subvert the gentlemanly role by wearing Mother's lingerie.

Boiler Room Door

As to the matter of paternal feelings, I didn't use the word "daughter" frequently, while "mother" was constantly in my mouth. The fact that anybody could see she was young enough to be my daughter did not bother me, in fact it touched me. But few had actually intimated that we were related. Is it because it is not uncommon for young women and older men to consort? In any case I would have welcomed their inquiry, because the public displaying of our relationship was a source of delight to me. Whatever their reasons might be for not calling her my "daughter," mine were simple enough: unlike my previous (and partly overlapping) relationship with my mother, my feelings for my daughter were so erotic, so exclusively addressed to the "woman" I discovered in her, that they overwhelmed my natural paternal affections. Or perhaps it would be more accurate to say that my paternal affections only increased my desire for her as a woman. She herself provoked this bias of my feelings for her. Sometimes, like a little cat, unexpectedly, she would dart her tongue out and lick my ear or my neck. At such moments, my emotion of desire was so intense that I teetered on the edge of a loss of control. I say "emotion" because it was not mere physical excitement but passionately intertwined tenderness and erotic violence. For that matter, I never had the urge to be violent with my mother, only gently filial—with the exception of the metaphorical violence of argument she drove me to. But with my girl—I intensely desired, and it was only desire that was involved—to slap and bite her while fucking, and only a supreme effort of self-control prevented me from doing so. She exercised no such control, as I have said, and many mornings I awoke with dark blue marks on my body. I shared with her this almost irresistible desire to hurt, because the hurting was a form of penetration, of physical possession, of extreme intimacy. For that matter, she could never really hurt me because any pain she inflicted was immediately transformed by some rearrangement of emotional molecules into intense pleasure! Why did we both experience such pleasure in hurting and in being hurt by the other? I think our infliction and acceptance of passionate pain was a pressing-through to some darker intimacy: the father-daughter relationship buried at the core of our erotic passion. She told me on more than one occasion that she felt homicidal towards me at these times. I understood.

Kitchen Door

The only "lies" I ever had to tell my sweet girl were my occasional transparent attempts to conceal the extent of my passion for her—because I became afraid not only that I was making myself too vulnerable, but even provoking that magnetic repulsion which had been my own reaction to my mother's overwhelming embrace. A form of self-preservation? But my more serious lies were the fabrications whereby I tried to make her believe I was less attached to my mother than was actually the case. Because the strangest reversal in this curious triangle was that, just as I had once hidden my guilty affair with my daughter from my mother (briefly: while I had hidden my relations with other women, I soon told her the truth about my passionate involvement with the girl), so now I had to disguise my entirely innocent relations with my mother from my daughter. And that was puzzling, because my daughter, unlike my mother, was quite impervious to jealousy. She couldn't care less if I talked to or looked at other women—in fact she told me that if I were to have a passing fling or go to a whore, she wouldn't even want to know about it. This of course made my passion for her all the more exclusive! Whereas my mother's grinding jealousy pushed me inexorably into the arms of what had at first been nonexistent "other women," and then . . . My girl only said, "As long as I am in your heart, it's ok." The only time I ever saw her jealous and even in a rage was when I left her over one Thanksgiving to take care of my mother who had had a minor fall and complained of chest pains. She told me that if I didn't get over my sickly dependence on my mother (but surely it was my mother who was dependent upon me! I thought), she would leave me. At the time I was deeply hurt and justifiably so, I thought, since I was only acting according to the dictates of my heart, but it wasn't so simple. After all, my mother had had innumerable crises of this sort—so many links in the chain that held me. It seems to me upon reflection that my mother's jealousy was sexual whereas my girl's was emotional; and that both were irrefutable. My dilemma was that I felt I should really be able to entertain them both (in the sense of holding both relationships entwined, of being able to satisfy them both because they were not mutually exclusive) because the emotion of tenderness and care was as real on the one hand as desire and passionate love on the other. Were the ancient jealousies of mother and daughter reignited through me? What did this mean? That my mother really wanted to be fucked and my daughter to be loved and protected? The oddest thing about this predicament, however, was that my sweet daughter, so free, so independent, so experimental, so—detached—was defiant and difficult about my innocent, neutral, if anxious concerns for my mother, while the latter, for twenty-five years raging against phantoms, now was apparently indifferent in the face of my passionate affair with the girl. More than that, she seemed to abstract herself from this humiliating intrusion, and to relate to me with a purity of womanly-maternal love—I later learned this was a deception and that she had never been purged of the old sexual demon of jealousy. Not that the division between emotion and erotic desire that had dominated my feelings for my mother persisted in my own soul—the sight of my girl's naked body, and particularly of the sweet slight swell of her belly and the black narrow furze beneath it, awoke an emotion so violent and so sweet in my heart that I thought I might die of it. The emotion coincided exactly with the desire.

Pantry Back Door

The pantry was the only room in the house with two doors: the first led into the pantry from the living/dining room, and the second, concealed by a large cupboard, was, quite unexpectedly, the back door leading out of the house. Taking my girl by the "back door" was a kind of ultimate carnal knowledge: an inner sanctum. I had dreamed of this physical intimacy throughout the years with my mother, but it was unmentionable because of the dirtiness it represented, which for her was the "dirtiness" of sex itself. Even after I had begun to wander among mother's proxies, I was never able to learn this secret. But my daughter offered herself to me in this way almost from the first day! When I pressed my way into her rear entrance, slowly inching in, guided by her hesitant, fearful, increasingly agitated and suddenly ecstatic and urgent instructions, gripped by the perianal muscles, I felt I was at last knowing the secret self of woman. I was a witness of her intense self-pleasure and loss of control. Whereas in normal intercourse she offered herself but could still play, remain aloof, be mistress of the occasion, in anal penetration she subjected herself willingly and wholly vulnerable, not as an equal partner in pleasure but separate and almost helpless as I mastered her and deliberately gave her the ambiguous pleasure and pain she desired, and took for myself supreme emotional and physical delight. At this depth of interiority, there was no more distinction between the emotion and the physical. What thrilled me beyond any pleasure was that my girl, with all the will and independence of mind of a strong woman, was submitting herself to me in trust and self-abandon; and that, my legs trembling and the sweat pouring down my face, was at the same time her instrument, a slave! And yet I could inflict this pain transmuted into pleasure with the most tender love for her, less aware of my own pleasure than of her savage, almost alien ecstasy. Interiority, within which my familial relationships had bloomed like a hothouse, was curiously both fulfilled and annulled at this point. The interiority I acceded to within my girl embodied for me the secret, the hidden dimension, of woman. And simultaneously she had opened for me the concealed door that led to the outside.

Part III

෧   MY SISTER MY SWEET WITCH   ෨

Onstage

Notwithstanding the rhapsodic tone of the above, this peculiar paternal affair flickered to an abrupt end almost from one day to the next. In spite of their daily fucking, it was as if I could never get enough of her. That is why she finally left me, I was convinced. "You're always grabbing me!" she complained. The episode with my daughter was brief in comparison to my mother's. The former outgrew me soon after "becoming a woman" thanks to my passionate ministrations (her assertion). It must also be admitted that she found my sentimental inability to overcome my feelings of guilt toward my mother intolerable—a relationship which appeared as foolish and out of place as a grandmother's obsession.

By the time my sister came back into my life, that early, maternal, crablike embrace had been finally loosened. My distant memories of her—almost my twin since less than nine months separated our birth days—had kept the fairytale eroticism of children's half-conscious games of sexual experimentation.

Although we were brother and sister, we had to re-make acquaintance. We had been separated for decades by the malicious spirit of my mother: first by her bodily presence which overwhelmed our childish loves; then by her ghostly absence which haunted us. And by my daughter? No, she had been an impossible fancy. She had carved a cross in my heart, but she hadn't mortgaged it like my mother. My heart continued to bleed from it. I would always love her like a daughter. After all, how else could I have had such a daughter whom I had always desired? I could only have dreamed of her. This story could have been told quite differently.

In particular I remember playing doctor with my sister and a little girlfriend, nine or ten years old like us, but far more delicate than us, both toughened by endless summers along the creek that ran through our land, catching crayfish, fooling around on the neighborhood farm switching flies off the cows' backs and stealing eggs, and down by the lake swimming and boating in an ancient rowboat. In fact, my sister had become a regular tomboy and my faithful pal. The neighbor's little girl, with her radiant yellow hair and timid if precocious nature, was the perfect victim (or "patient") offered up for my and my nurse's fascinated exploration. This was accomplished by having the child stretch out on a cot in the cabin next to the boathouse, and then clumsily unbutton her blouse and pull up her skirt in order to examine her tiny titties and her hairless pudenda, all of which was done with medical aplomb, through the insertion of a straw and then either looking down or applying one's ear to it, or blowing through it. This I did with tremulous excitement as my little sister-nurse assisted me by passing the straws and peering over my shoulder, until it was her turn to play patient. Much less selfless than our little girlfriend, my sister's alarmed protestations could only be overcome by my—and the former patient's—wounded denunciations of unfairness. Even then she would only allow the procedure after her hands were pried away from her private parts by me and my enthusiastic new nurse. And there were other occasions, for instance, the day we walked barefoot down the tree-lined road above the lake's shore, she panted and called out trying to catch up as I skipped ahead. I had felt an odd twinge, and suddenly slowed down and called for her to hurry up and see what I had in my pocket. My penis was as wriggly as an eel and I had a hole in a pocket: come on, I said, put your hand in my pocket. She glanced suspiciously at me, and I said, I have a candy for you there, at which she shoved her hand brusquely into my pocket and felt through the hole and squealed in dismay and ran off as I collapsed, laughing and rolling about in the grass.

As she grew into puberty and beyond, my fascination with her sex grew with her. I would spy on her whenever I could, in her bath or when they changed to go swimming. She seemed oblivious of my passionate interest—but was she? I wondered, for I was quite incapable of concealing its outward manifestations. Once I had climbed into a tree in order to observe as she undressed for her bath, not thinking to draw the curtains of the bathroom window on the dark country night. From thirty feet away I saw the brightly illuminated spectacle as she ran her bath and undressed, caressing her surprisingly (to me) full breasts and bent over, swinging them both in her cupped palms. What invisible audience was she playing for? I wondered. It was at this thrilling moment that I came violently and slipped with a crash out of my ten-foot high perch. She must have heard something, because my last glance caught her alarmed stare out the window into the dark and a protective hand and forearm about her breasts. This was in fact the last time I enjoyed my sister vicariously at that tender age, since I became involved with my mother shortly after. My experiences with my mother had "bracketed" my amorous but make-believe attempts on my sister, both preceding them in my childhood as well as following them in my boyhood, as has been seen.

My Self

I have hesitated to reveal my self here, because what follows is in the present. I seem to fluctuate in and out of identity. What can I tell you about my sister at this late, "second" stage of our lives? She routed me. I was entirely unfamiliar with her adult, female force when I met her. It had been so many years since I had last seen her. Now, however, decades later, after I had taken the first tentative steps to contact her—I was met at first with reluctance and suspicion on her part. She had raised an entire family by then, a life which I had been absent from, ensnared in the coils of my mother-lover. When she finally suggested that we meet, however, the roles appeared to have been reversed. When I thought to seduce her, I was instead overwhelmed by her orgasmic violence. That bright summer's day when we finally met again, she was engaged in lively conversation, her turned-up lascivious little fox's nose, the laughter on her lips, parted, suggestive—well, my cock pointed straight up at her inside my pants. I swear that it pointed in her direction, as if it recognized her before I did. She had changed completely, she had become a woman—that mystery I had wrestled with all my life. From what she told me later, her vagina went wet at the same moment, as if awoken by memories of our childhood. Need I say that on the same evening when we had found each other again, my sister and I bedded down together? The few friends who surrounded us knew when it was time to retire discretely. Of course they didn't know about our familial relationship. I had told them that my sister was a relative, nothing more. I don't know what she had told them. I was surprised by my speed. I think I wanted to make up for those years apart: as if the stretching apart of the past could only be released abruptly, like elastic drawn out to the snapping point. Now we both snapped back. Her body was the first surprise. Instead of my mother's body which had aged ahead of mine and begged for pity (to my mind, not hers!), instead of my daughter's which was fresh as a pumpkin and elicited unrequited craving, my sister's body was like mine, with its defects and its beauties, the weight of its years and mysteriously contemporaneous with my own—I had never been with a woman of my generation before! Doubly my generation, you might say, almost my twin. Our familiarity was perfect, as if we had known each other from the womb. When she licked the first milky drop from the tip of my cock that night and I drank from her cup, we were exchanging the original liquor that had nourished us both. When my cock pumped her, it was, she said, as if it were her cock entering me: which end belonged to whom? That doesn't mean that the immediate intimacy between us allayed my fears and suspicions and even terror of women. In fact, after that first night of passionate love-making, I had a horrifying dream: I dreamed I awoke from this night of love in the arms of a stunted woman with pock-marked face who grinned maliciously at me, gleefully announcing that she had infected me with multiple diseases. In bed with us was a man who was totally intoxicated, perhaps comatose. Was he also me? Terror-struck I fled, pursued by some faceless dread. Was she a witch?

THE PERSONAE

After all she was my sister—even closer than a mother or a daughter, like another self of myself. Wasn't this the ultimate prohibition? We knew each other erotically as well as we knew ourselves. Although I thought I had devised a strategy to seduce her, none was required. She needed only to suck me into her psyche. Even now, as I write, the fire runs down my sternum and empties my chest. *Sartor resartus.* Filleted. Cock stripped down like a sausage. Body turned inside out like a glove by her tender, cunning, skillful, practiced fingers. Our love was so self-identifying it was masturbatory! My sister raped me with the sweetest tenderness! When she would begin to caress me in delicate curves on chest and stomach, her fingers drew my cock irresistibly upwards like a serpent. And for the first time in this peculiar family of interlocking lusts, each of us fully assumed the persona caught in this love. That is, she consciously enjoyed the desire of a sister for her brother and I the lust of a brother for his sister. I mean that while my mother had indulged her passionate desire for a son in me, she also repudiated the suggestion that I be anything but a Spanish gentleman, a *caballero*, for whom she would always be a blushing romantic bride. She was never able to accept the twenty-one years of difference between our ages, and deeply resented my young man's "silliness" and casual ways.

And my darling daughter really wanted, I finally realized, the morally authoritative and superior father I had never been—even though she had at first desired her father as lover *sur les bords.* The former was a source of endless irritation for me, and the latter, of enduring agony. Paradoxically, much to my astonishment, in the end mother and daughter wanted the same, dignified, mature man—and it wasn't me, my labyrinthine self! For my part, the familial dimension complicated, and at first rendered more interesting, and so compensated for the lack of any enduring desire for my mother's collapsing body. Whereas with my daughter, my increasing realization of the nature of her childish dependence and need gave rise in *loco parentis* to a tender, paternalistic indulgence of the slackening of erotic intensity on her part. Yet I was haunted towards the end of our relationship by the similarities of her attitudes—a look of boredom, an impatient withdrawal from a caress—with those I had shown my mother, oblivious to her signals of desire. For there is no doubt that after the first savage passions of courtship, once she had secured the father she craved, the relationship tipped back into a sexless filial one. My anguish, like my mother's, flooded up with my "child's" loss of interest.

It's true that at this later stage of our lives, there was no blatant age difference to betray the nature of our relationship, no suspicion arose spontaneously in the minds of acquaintances and friends. And since we had been separated for so many years because of the circumstances of my education abroad, and our mother's deliberate and successful undertaking to separate me from the rest of the family, our sister-brother intimacy had been dispelled, and a certain adult distance or suspicion had come between us, so that the suffocating closeness I had experienced with the other two women in my family was dispelled here. Finally, when I moved to Paris to set up house with her, her circle of friends had no suspicion that I was her brother—I had taken my mother's maiden name when I was coupled with her, and my daughter and I had felt no compulsion to share knowledge of our relationship with others. Now, sometimes, a friend would remark on the extraordinary resemblance between my sister and myself, not so much physical—she took after our father while I took after our mother—but temperamentally: we appeared to be twins. As a result we could wear our family bond with a delicious complicity, without any sort of misgivings vis-à-vis our social circle. We couldn't resist, however, telling them that by a remarkable coincidence I was born on the same day and the same year as her brother and she in the same year as my sister.

I won't conceal that for the first weeks or even months my overpowering lust for her was met by a proportionate terror. Was it because no unbridgeable distance separated me from the female, now? It made me wonder if I had entered into the previous family relationships because they were safely conducted on either side of an abyss! Being on an equal, horizontal plane, this woman was no longer split from me on the reassuring, vertical, generational axis. Geometry aside, I think a rage now drove me along the horizontal axis of desire, an ever-increasing and insatiable erotic appetite for constantly renewed couplings and the invention of freshly perverse acts, the purpose of which was awareness through sharpened pleasure: a redoubled lucidity regarding the nature of my body and its separation from my sister's, or an unclouded perception of what it meant to be "other." Was this the secret of my sexual madness? Even among ordinary couples the other tends to merge with one's self sexually in an unconscious identification, flowing out of ancient childhood emotions. So in order to love, I had first consciously to identify with the female, as such—coupling with mother or daughter or sister,—and then to possess her as fully other than myself with excruciatingly sweet awareness. Exacerbated pleasure, it seemed to me, came from overcoming that inescapable and acute perception of her as a part or extension of myself, in order to come to recognize her as totally *other* than the self. In that orgasmic moment came ecstatic enjoyment! Is that unclear? It was the explicit awareness that she was so tightly bound to myself by the root, by quasi-identity, that rendered an exquisite intensity of recognition of her as utterly separate in the friction of skin and moisture, and especially in her orgasms when she floated entirely out of my reach and into her own mental body.

Being the Same As Being the Other

In our ecstatic and wild dancing at parties and clubs and at our own notorious parties in Paris, in the fluid extension of our bodies together into a social dimension, friends and even strangers could observe an unusually intimate camaraderie and erotic spontaneity between us. Sometimes I would ask her to insert a Chinese sex-toy, little linked spheres, in her vagina when we went out together, so that I could imagine their rotations and her helplessness when we danced. Without telling her, I would pull her skirt up behind as we rocked, revealing her thighs and her panties. Knowing her, however, I suspected that she realized it all along. At other times I would ask her to wear no panties on such occasions, just the garter belt and black stockings over her very white legs. My heart beat crazily during these public spectacles and my cock would swell embarrassingly in my pants.

Having always had an exhibitionistic streak myself, when I exhibited her in this surreptitious manner, it was as exciting as if I had translated the spectacle of her into one of myself. This smooth reciprocity of the signs, or reversal of the arrows, of erotic love applied to all the varieties of our love-making. The univocal character of the sexual imagination which had applied to my earlier relations—the masochistic lusts I had developed with Mother, being tied and molested and beaten, then the sadistic reversal with my daughter, which she initiated with her desire to be mock-raped, anally penetrated, and my wild attempts to bind her—now imploded in a frenzied fluctuation of these modes in my lust for my sister. On our honeymoon in New Orleans, for the first time I tied Sister up to the wrought-iron backing of our elaborate bed, her hands fastened to the top railing as she half sat, half lay back, legs spread wide and ankles roped to the foot of the bed. She wore a red bustier and red garter belt and stockings and nothing else. I proceeded to "molest" her as she played the part of the ingénue, subjecting her to slow caresses from her ears to her toes, and penetrated her with various implements and finally with tongue and cock until she came, screaming. Her noisy orgasms were always a source of delight to me, and I would imagine neighbors and guests in the house pricking up their ears. Similarly, I would have her tie me up and I writhed with the kicks and penetrations of her red-patent, leather, stiletto pumps until my groans burst into shouts. This total lack of vocal control was something new to me, and her ability to unleash it astonishing. I could no longer withhold any part of myself in sexual intercourse. Even our male and female roles became quite relative, after we started to use a double dildo with two rubber phalluses, perhaps suggested by her frequent references to my "cute ass," a very male expression of desire. I was shy, feeling like a virgin in this regard, reluctant to reveal my own inverted and answering lusts, but tremulous with longing and shaken by ancient contradictory emotions. She responded to my childish reticence with curiosity and sisterly lasciviousness, and dressing up in the most feminine and graceful lingerie, she strapped on the dildo, the stubby end plugged inside her vagina, placed me in that most female of positions, the doggie crouch on elbows and knees, ass up and head down, and proceeded to bugger me (as she called it) with the second, long phallus, slowly, daintily, and the orgasm induced when she put hand to cock sent a shuddering down my groin hitherto unknown to me. I became pliant and female under her touch, and we both experienced homosexual emotions for the other—I the female and she the male. In our play I became the sister and she the brother!

Jealousy, Insecurity, Pain

My filial emotions for my mother were finally dispelled. She had not only denied me my inheritance from my father, but even established a trust fund in a happily compliant relative's name, which would leave me penniless in case of her prior decease. This was her vengeance against the young man who had left her for a girl who might be her granddaughter! She would never forgive him for that betrayal and would never speak to him again, nor communicate in writing for the rest of her life.

The same, however, was not true regarding my relationship with my daughter. However happy my sister made me, however delightful a companion and sweet a whore she was to me, I could not get over my remorse at having "abandoned" my "little girl" as I sentimentally thought of her, now reduced to a purely paternal relationship. I helped her monetarily in any way I could, until the measures my mother took had reduced me to poverty. No matter how often I told myself that my attitude was mere self-indulgence, that my daughter was a strong and capable woman quite able to take care of herself, I would be overcome by pity and fear for her, guilty over my paternal failure, my inadequacy to provide for her, to watch over her—to protect her, in a word. I no longer felt any desire for her, but the frustration of not being able to care for her tormented me. She was my cub, my baby, and our separation left wounds on my psychic body that would not heal. It didn't make it easier that my sister, endlessly indulgent and kind to me, had no sympathy for my ex-lover but only scorn—insecurity, I felt, over my anxiety for my daughter. In fact, the only friction in our lives together arose from my unceasing compulsion to somehow provide for my girl—instead of "letting her live her life," as my sister put it—and her consequent bitterness over my deep emotional dependency on my former lover, which appeared to reproduce with her now the same dual relationship as when I had lived with my daughter and had been afflicted over my mother.

A dark wave would submerge me in despondency again and I would remain immersed in pain until it could be alleviated through fresh reassurance of my daughter's well-being. This introduced some distrust between me and my sister, insubstantial as a shadow and unfounded I felt. There was no betrayal of my lover (my sister, now) in my preoccupation with my daughter, but my sister's resentment of it only increased my pain—and my anger over behavior which seemed gratuitous and heartless. I wanted there to be no subterfuge with my sister, I had entered into what I felt to be a free relationship with huge relief, but her indignation whenever I declared my wish to provide moral or material help for my former lover only pushed me into concealing these harmless intentions, whereas I wished on the contrary to share them with her (or I thought I did?)!

Then her outraged reactions to these deceptions led me to the inexorable conclusion that each of these women, who might as well represent various female potentialities for a man, was prepared to accept only an exclusive relationship, not just physically, but far more importantly on the *emotional* plane. While I could understand the possessiveness and murderous vindictiveness of my mother and the plaintive helplessness of my daughter, this same need for exclusiveness on the part of my comrade and sister was deeply puzzling. It must, I felt, be rooted in a universal female nature! Abhorrent as such a conclusion could only be to my ethic of dispossession, it was demonstrated most patently by my sister, precisely because she, who had made her life entirely on her own with irresistible energy and a diamond-sharp mind, at this emotional level did not differ qualitatively from my mother or my daughter. It was, I thought, as if each of them deliberately—or helplessly—exposed the most vulnerable nerve instead of concealing it: my mother, her narcissistic physical jealousy; my daughter her emotional insecurity; my sister—her devouring need to be loved.

All Her Rolls

I and my sister had agreed early on in our renewed sexual relationship that theatre, *mises en scene*, scenarios, were an intrinsic dimension of our love-life. Whereas I had always remained on the brittle edges of fantasy with my mother, more consciously with my daughter, with my sister I felt I had entered decisively onto that open stage which until then had looked out through windows or half-open doors. I and she not only absorbed the roles of siblings fully, but practiced with complete freedom the perversions, the sexual inventions, the erotic play which such roles permitted, even encouraged. The brother-sister intimacy and camaraderie didn't channel our erotic impulses in a single direction, like the masochistic passions of the mother/son relationship or the sadistic, even rapist aggressiveness with my daughter and her lust for self-pollution. Brother and sister could exchange phantomatic identities, and as lascivious pals could push each other to reciprocal perversions. Our easy intimacy had become the condition that made our theatre of sex possible. Each provided his or her own inventions: I was more interested in the physical details of the props and costumes, while she was drawn to the situation, the scenarios. We would discuss the characters which each would assume— my sister had a cast of seven female types, each quite different from the others, which would evoke corresponding personae on my part. The erotic for us became theatre, and this meant that it was played out somewhere between the real dimension of who we both were, and the unreal dimension of our invented situations and characters: for example, the "Submissive Little Maid" scenario. She would dress in a tiny, demure, white apron and a filmy white blouse. She wore the daintiest of white panties under the apron, and white stockings with a girlish, pink-ribboned garter belt. Beneath the filmy blouse she wore nothing, so that her taut nipples caught up the light material. She also did her hair up in pigtails and dabbed a little too much pink lipstick on. When I arrived in my black corduroy suit and with serious mien, she addressed me only as "sir," in a meek voice and with downcast eyes, and told me the mistress had instructed her to do everything the master required.

I addressed her in a paternalistic tone, stern but affectionate, and her name was "Little Sissy." A pat on her bottom in its skimpy panties was playfully indulgent. It's true that seeing her large breasts shift inside the blouse, and her plump bottom swing to the radio music, and watching her frequent bending over to clean up around the place which displayed her crotch (was it entirely unconscious and innocent? wondered my paternalistic character) had the no-doubt unintentional and after all harmless consequence of producing a considerable erection inside my pants, which of course I concealed out of concern for her tender and innocent nature. After she served me my five o'clock cocktail, I kindly invited her to have half a glass for herself and to sit beside me so that we could have a fatherly chat and discuss her duties. Was it my voyeuristic fault or some juvenile mischievousness on her part that sitting in that brief apron with her knees spread displayed the narrow white furrow of the childish panties that barely covered her pubic mound? When she left to get something in the kitchen, flouncing her protruding behind as she walked, I took out my cock quickly to inspect its change of state I had noticed during the chat, and surely enough it was slick with an unprovoked (by the innocent child) emission. She came back with another bottle and must have caught sight of my stiff member, although I covered it quickly with my hand in an attempt to shield her girlish innocence. She looked away and then glanced into my face with shy reproach, and I said it was all right, dear, it was just that I had to check it. This is said without any gauche attempt at the pornographic, but merely to illustrate the theatrical and detached manner in which my sister and I interacted. She was entirely unlike my real daughter, who finally had assumed a passive role toward me, taking me for the fatherly and authoritative character she actually wanted—in other words played her part—just as my mother had played hers, and forced me to play mine willy-nilly. Here the part played was unconstrained and wholly inventive, my sister playing a daughterly character, which was not hers in reality . . .

When I tied loops of rope around her breasts causing them to swell out over the top of the blouse, and tied her feet apart while she was in a standing position, with her apron tucked into her garter belt and her panties pulled down around her knees, and pulled her arms up and tied her hands to an improvised balcony at the mezzanine level in our house, I was so excited that my knees trembled, and she! Her legs quaked uncontrollably while I caressed and penetrated her with dildos and finger and finally my own burning member. She came with shouts and a speed uncustomary for her, and I had to catch her, collapsing in my arms, and untie her, she was so overcome. This was only possible because of the fullness of trust and freedom between us. In between these staged episodes, she would sometimes ask me to make love to her "Hollywood style," which meant minus any of our scenarios or props, with romantic passion and straight up and down sex. However, it is indicative of the depth of her own engagement with the theatrical that even when she was asking me for non-fantasized sex, the reference she used was "Hollywood," the ultimate celluloid illusion! For my part, enjoyment of sex was doubled through these theatrical representations. They brought me such extreme excitement that my emotions bordered on complete loss of control, and gave me concern for my psychic balance. I began to believe that I had become addicted, and would actually pine for, say, Little Sissy, even if she only existed in our joint imaginations; or for "Sadie," the character of the domineering mother, which she played with equal aplomb, and whose scorn and coldly erotic punishments I lusted for.

Playing Herself: Nakedness

So my sister played a dozen roles, roles pertaining to submissive daughter or to domineering mother, and each of these of course evoked corresponding roles on my part: paternalistic, punishing, or else filial and submissive. When she acted the sisterly role, it seemed to bring home to her with most poignancy the actual relationship she was involved in. For example, one role she proposed for the sister-figure she really was (i.e., a sister playing a sister) was her ritual shaving and an erotic dessert. In this role my sister dressed in a normal teenager's frock with white cotton panties and a wooly sweater, with a lift-bra and—bobby socks! The role couldn't be played very often, at most once every few weeks, because of obvious physical limitations (the slowness of hair growth). We would discuss very precisely and explicitly our roles and scenario before initiating a scene, in order to augment the tension. This particular scene began by leading the "sister" to the bidet and seating her there after pulling down her panties. These remained about her ankles, and I turned on the warm water, as she faintly protested, and I reassured her with older-brother authority, telling her that this was all the rage among the college girls. Then soaping the *mons veneris* I carefully shaved the pubic hair from around her vagina, leaving just a hint at the top. In spite of the innumerable times we had played the most varied sexual games, I had never touched her body with such intimacy as on these occasions. Being apprehensive of the exceedingly delicate physiology of this core of her body, and intent on shaving off every little curl, I had to roll and smooth down and draw out every dip and fold and rise of her *mons* and outer *labia*. Her legs trembled as I did so, and I administered slight, cunning caresses as I shaved her. When she was entirely denuded, I told her to stand in front of the mirror holding her skirts up, so that I could dry about the vagina gently and thoroughly. Why is it that her cunt, stripped of its protective cover, produced such a powerful sense of obscenity in its reflection? Perhaps because it revealed her desire to expose herself totally, without the faintest restraint? And in fact I felt that this gift of herself without adornment, in all the vulnerability of her exposed sex, was the mark of the most extreme sisterly love. What I had not been prepared for, being driven by sheer lust, was the tender emotion which the sight of her pink, little-girl crevice gave rise to. Her psychic force was such that it seemed to modify the appearance of her *pudenda*! I was astonished and could not take my eyes off it. This act which we had shared, and which might appear to some to be gratuitous, was a ritual which sealed our brother-and-sister pact. It had resurrected childhood events with all the mystery and terror and delight these had held.

I led her to the bed that I had prepared in advance, a white sheet stretched over it, a dessert spoon on one side of the bed, and a container of ice cream next to it. She stripped naked—this was one of the few roles in which full nakedness was essential, her shaved sex making her appear more naked than naked. My feelings about her body, which this theatre of total exposure touched on, were entirely different from those concerning my mother or my daughter. Regarding my mother it was simple enough: a still-beautiful ruin. As the years with her passed, I became conscious of the deterioration of what had once been a perfect body: since I looked at her with the eyes of a boy at first and then a young man, I couldn't help but notice—although I didn't want to, not out of distaste but out of pity—the merciless drag of time on her face and body. And this created a distance between us, a gap which I grieved over, and which to her of course was unbearable. With my daughter, on the contrary, I had practiced an almost pagan idolatry of her flawless body. As a result I was detached and voyeuristic. In my sister, however, I recognized the same bodily imperfections, the reality and the sensuality of the flesh we shared. The camaraderie of our brother-and-sister condition made our erotic sharing entirely unselfconscious and, seemingly, unlimited.

I stretched out her arms and legs in spread-eagle fashion, and tied her hands and feet to the corner posts gently. I then proceeded to serve a helping of ice cream onto her vagina, which I began by eating with the spoon, and concluded by licking up the cream directly before it melted down between her quaking labia. She insisted on tasting the ice cream herself from the tip of my cock, and so we supped on each other. Before it was all gone, I dipped my own hot implement inside her still creamy, cool interior, as she begged me to. This sharing of ice cream in particular evoked our childhood hijinx.

On Show

The theatrical dimension was heightened if an audience could witness our staging. For that reason, usually without letting her know, I would leave a curtain partly open during our nightly showings, so that if somebody from the building across the street happened to glance over, they couldn't miss what was going on in our brightly-lit apartment, all glass on both sides on the top floor of our *hôtel particulier*. Often I carefully positioned her so that an intimate part of her body would be well lit: for example, once when she straddled me as I sat, I delicately pulled up her gossamer dress behind so that her white ass riding me would be plainly visible. I am sure my sister realized that I was setting her up, and played along for her own pleasure, deriving amusement from my ignorance of her awareness. Consciousness, heightened awareness, was the core of our erotic excitement. This multiple seeing of her through anonymous eyes was intoxicating. The more we staged the scene, the more incontrovertible it became to me that the exquisite pleasure we derived from these games was only minimally related to the physical—essentially it was the undeniable appearing of the body, yet its absence in the mental representation of my sister. This "theatre" was the medium which enabled the sharpest focus of the reality of my lover, or more accurately, that my lover was other than myself. The metaphysics, which I felt I could almost grasp in the reflection of myself in her eyes, the seeing of myself through her eyes, was the deepest source of pleasure, even of ecstasy. Paradoxically, it was when the pleasure of the "flesh" was at its most intense— almost disorienting, because I could see, feel, taste myself through her perception of me, a perception made radical by the extreme nature of our mutual provocations—that my member no longer seemed to be mine but some foreign, organic artifact which yielded the exchange of pleasure between us. For example, her prolonged tasting of it appeared to me to be a symbiotic feast linking us—so that I looked on with her at this spectacle, tasting it with her, fascinated by its extraordinary reverberations throughout my body, and for a few moments "stood outside" myself in ecstatic contemplation.

It occurs to me now that, although we relate very exactly in our brother-sister roles as comrades and accomplices, and while she could play every kind of character with equal delight and lubricity, she always waits for me to suggest which of her characters I want her to assume, what staging we should prepare, what props and which scene we should play each night. So the underlying role which appears to be fundamental for her is that of the woman-as-recipient. Make no mistake—she constructs the characters and assembles the scenery and props with as much or more intensity than I. In fact, looking back on my own characters, I realize that these arise largely in response to the hallucinatory harem, the erotic modalities, imagined in response to the carefully delineated scenarios I request. In fact, it's in these inventions, our familial theatre, that the clearest projection of our brother-sister collaboration lies. I have been using the present tense in this last paragraph, because my sister and I are together in the present, and we shall soon be sketching out our next scenario. This morning, together in the shower, I pissed between the cheeks of her ass with my heart in my throat, and when she turned around the little stream splashed onto her naked pubic mound. I had waited for her to wake up and go to her shower for half an hour, with a pressing need to take a piss, but the wait—even the wait!—was unbearably exciting . . .

Tomorrow evening, when we go out dancing at the *Coupole,* I'll ask her to play the role of the cynical young tease, Bobbsie, who knows every trick in the book to titillate her older suitor. She will conceal on—or more accurately in—her person her favorite erotic toy. I'll shave her before going out and she will wear a dress which is quite revealing, with little slashes cut out by the designer about the ass and the thighs, and she will not be allowed to wear panties. Her and my favorite scenes are those we perform in public. It's as if our characters fully become us only when we are performing on a stage.

Sacred Theatre

I can no longer escape the conclusion that these family relationships constituted an obsessive theatre—one that inheres in the very nature of such relationships. Whether with Mother or Daughter or Sister, such love is obsessive and requires histrionic representation. That is, by nature it is so dramatic and peculiar that it can only be theatrical—seen against the backdrop of everyday life. Not only is it deeply rooted in the condition of men and women, but is also purely artificial. Each one of us—I and my sister right now—feels the need to heighten the artifice of prop and scene and character, i.e., to play our role beyond ourselves. To dramatize ourselves, in a word. To enhance our relationship, our being. To make a spectacle of ourselves. But the converse is also true. Theatre is our true home, where we belong, where we are relevant—in my theatre, that is! And theatre by definition is not—and can not be—part of the real world. As noted above, even my sister yields the direction of our little theatre to me . . . If Mother and Daughter cannot help but construe their relations to Son and Father in the most dramatic "strobe-light," the most exotic stage-set, they are at the same time severely constrained by the mold of their specific family roles—these are univocal. But between my sister and me no such constraint exists! As co-equals and in complicity, we can invent any theatre, not merely one modeled on the sister-brother couple. And we do! I play her father, her servant, her abusive pimp, her sexually deviant adolescent to be severely chastised, and she plays mistress and mother, ingénue and daughter, dominatrix, courtesan, and sister. In fact she plays mother, sister and daughter roles indifferently! She collects all the roles into herself. And since she leaves the direction of the theatre to me—well, essentially I create the roles and scenarios, with her passionate—or indulgent?—collaboration. This has become our theatre of desire, that is, since these family relations subtend the forms of sexual desire. Hence my sister and I indulge our every erotic whim in this play—just as we recognize the stage upon which our relations are founded.

It was only very recently that I realized that my relationships with Mother, Daughter—and a fortiori with Sister—were exclusively theatrical. Not in the limited sense set forth above, but because, while each had to invent their exotic roles, I alone held intercourse with all three family members on this plane. Each one of them had to deal only with me, as they were (or resolved to be) mutually exclusive. And I had to reinvent each of them. It is true that I had the complicity of my sister who assumed all our roles, in fact I sometimes almost doubted the reality of those earlier relationships, so sharp was the focus and definition of my sister as she put on (and took off) one persona after the other like a piece of intimate apparel. Perhaps her duplicity and her paranoid intensity of personality outreached the others? I was often aware of the clumsiness of my own role-playing in the face of her persuasive, incarnated roles. Even while I initiated the perverse games, I was overcome by the sexual power of each of her personae. Was I lapsing into idolatry?

৵

The nightmare I had dreamed after that first night of love with her—was it my terror of woman? And wasn't this terror rooted in the family mechanism which I had so thoughtlessly spawned in my imagination. In each of these "dreams" I reinvented the goddess Woman of whom I am the son, the father and the brother. Why is it that I appear to be destroyed by them? Is this the final stage? the abyss of pleasure? Are all my inventions of love, woman as sister, as mother, as daughter, destructive ghosts in the end? The pleasure is real, isn't it? That at least is real. I remember thinking, when I was with Mother, that every day that I had obtained the sexual grounding of pleasure by escaping into some other female, reality had been achieved. What a peculiar idea! Erotic escape into the *nada*. Saint John of the Cross, perverted. And it didn't change with my daughter, and still less with my sister, who provides me with sensual delight on demand, my sweet, ever-indulgent, lascivious, flaming-haired witch! The problem inherent in this erotic resolution of life is that it must be endlessly repeated. Pleasure vanishes within seconds of its orgasmic realization—however intense! To be grounded in this ecstatic pleasure (yes, outside oneself, in the female) is a contradiction in terms, it needs to be reenacted constantly. The soul is not touched by pleasure. Perhaps emptied a little more, each time, into the flesh. What I had thought to be a theatre of desire created by myself is perhaps a ritual of the absorption of my male energies and pretensions, a suction and swallowing of myself by the female, which I, brother or son or father, am, is, the supplicant of: *ascesis*.

Listen! I think my sister, Woman, is about to arrive. Then I will be able to inveigle, to con, to spank, to lick, to dog, to hump, to nose, to realize the myriad pressures and seductions and fantasies of "the man" whose sister, mother, and daughter she is: whose goddess she is.

Sacrifice of the Goddess

Still, I wasn't born yesterday! I mean, I've survived the wounds of intimate relations with two female members of my family, I think I know a little something now. Consequently, I have suggested to my sister several times that we go to a *particular* club. Finally, after she had lost a couple of pounds and felt that her curvaceous and seductive forms were just right for my plan, which she had already divined (she always knew in advance, whatever my cunning), she agreed. Preparations, costume, were discussed in detail. We decided she would wear an open-nipple bra (or I proposed and she disposed), and the most delicate and expensive and minute *Perla* panties I was able to buy her. The usual garter belt with black stockings which had become a quasi-religious habit (I found the black against her pale skin especially troubling). I also asked her to insert her favorite toy, the Chinese linked balls. A light blouse and jacket, and a skirt which unzipped to the hip, completed her costume. The obvious occurred to me as I "dressed" her—that costumes had always been for the women, even if I tried to oblige them now and then with a Japanese kimono or some leather thong under-wear for myself. For that matter, the roles played were tailored to the female partner—I was only a shadow-figure in all this! I had always been acutely conscious, with my sister, that her role-playing was agile, articulate, whereas mine was somewhat forced and clumsy.

As we drove to the club in St. Denis, I pulled her dress up over her thighs and buried my fingers in her velvet flesh, while we both pretended not to notice the astonished stares of the occasional passing driver. By the time we got to the club she was wet and my member was burning. The club entrance was elaborate with fake Moorish grilles on the windows and an interior décor done in sultanesque style with archways and arabesques. After paying a stiff entrance fee, an obsequious employee showed us down the heavily carpeted hallway to the main bar, and pointed out the corridors which led to the locker room, to the sauna and the hammam, and to the various "special" rooms (dungeon, massage, etc.). My sister walked close to me, a little tremulous, and I steered her by the elbow. The setting appeared quite conventional, with three or four couples seated about the gaudy glass bar with its interior red lighting, which bathed the customers in a dim but flattering glow. Large cushions were scattered around the corners of the room. We sat down on the stools and ordered white wine, and taking a closer look at the other guests, noticed that one of the women had a breast hanging outside her stylishly low-cut jacket, her nipple being caressed attentively by a much older, white-haired man. Another woman's dress was pushed up above her thighs, and her boyish companion had a hand lodged between them. The other two couples were ogling the latter over their drinks. Their eyes turned to us briefly, and then went back to the spectacle. I leaned over and gave my sister a kiss on the cheek to reassure her, and on impulse pulled up the zipper of her dress, so that the skirt fell open revealing most of one long leg sheathed in black stockings below the buckles and straps of a black-lace garter belt. She did nothing to cover it again, and my cock rose in my pants at the sight of it—but especially at the sight of the sight we were offering. We had the attention of the audience now, who glanced in our direction expectantly. Not wishing to disappoint them, I placed a hand on the tender white flesh at the top and inside of her thigh, thus displacing the garment and revealing her pale, shaven crotch. My sister, never one to be outdone, leaned forward and unzipped my fly, carefully extracting my cock. My heart was pounding uncomfortably and my face must have been flushed. My cock stood up ramrod stiff, held delicately between her fingers. We had not discussed in advance what we would actually do at the club (except agreeing we would make no exchange with other couples), so that I had no cues at this point. Eyes half-closed as she handled it, she appeared oblivious to what she was doing, in the innocence of dreaming; the purity of her womanly expression moved me. I stood up as if drawn to my feet by wires, and by now the other two couples were standing watching and I was vaguely aware that more people had entered the room from behind. My fingers were inside her now, and she was already wet, so moistening my cock's head further with saliva, I stepped between her thighs, swiveling her slightly on her stool so that her back rested against the padded bar. There was a surrounding murmur, people had come up behind us now, my sister's eyes were closed and she leaned back in complete abandon, her thighs spread wide, and I looked down at my thrusting member as if it were not mine, just some soft machinery, as it nudged the Chinese balls inside her. I forced myself to look up and into the eyes of the women in the group, and my heart jumped and my member seemed to swell, as if I were having sex with all of them. The fingers of a woman standing behind me slipped inside my loosened pants and down between the cheeks. A man reached in front of me and pulled aside my sister's blouse exposing a breast with its nipple protruding rigidly through the open slit of the bra, and he licked it avidly. My sister opened her eyes for the first time and looked not into my eyes but into the face of the man caressing her, and she began to groan with that loud, helpless, orgasmic violence I knew so well. I could hear the make-believe complaints at that long-ago childhood scene by the lake as our neighbor's little girl and I pried her open. We looked into each other's eyes with tranquil consciousness. I had felt the rush of blood through my chest with her first groan, and with the unknown woman's finger stirring inside me, I came in huge orgasmic bursts, unable to stop my cries. We "came to" after coming together—a score of people were in the room and they started applauding. We pulled our moistened clothes on hastily. I took her hand and led her in a rush back up the hallway hardly knowing where I was going, and we were let out by the obsequious and now appreciative attendant who whispered to me as we left, bravo, come again soon, Monsieur Dame, at half price! And we walked into the cool air of the evening, and I looked at her and she looked at me, The price for coming is not at all high, I said, and we began laughing and were hysterical with laughter by the time we reached the car. As we got in and drove back home I remember thinking that for the first time we had not been acting any familial part, we had merely been acting ourselves! I gave a glance at her still-flushed face in the darkened wings.

"Quite a performance." I murmured, half to myself, half to her.

SELECTED DALKEY ARCHIVE PAPERBACKS

PETROS ABATZOGLOU, *What Does Mrs. Freeman Want?*
PIERRE ALBERT-BIROT, *Grabinoulor.*
YUZ ALESHKOVSKY, *Kangaroo.*
FELIPE ALFAU, *Chromos.*
    Locos.
IVAN ÂNGELO, *The Celebration.*
    The Tower of Glass.
DAVID ANTIN, *Talking.*
ALAIN ARIAS-MISSON, *Theatre of Incest.*
DJUNA BARNES, *Ladies Almanack.*
    Ryder.
JOHN BARTH, *LETTERS.*
    Sabbatical.
DONALD BARTHELME, *The King.*
    Paradise.
SVETISLAV BASARA, *Chinese Letter.*
MARK BINELLI, *Sacco and Vanzetti Must Die!*
ANDREI BITOV, *Pushkin House.*
LOUIS PAUL BOON, *Chapel Road.*
    Summer in Termuren.
ROGER BOYLAN, *Killoyle.*
IGNÁCIO DE LOYOLA BRANDÃO, *Teeth under the Sun.*
    Zero.
BONNIE BREMSER, *Troia: Mexican Memoirs.*
CHRISTINE BROOKE-ROSE, *Amalgamemnon.*
BRIGID BROPHY, *In Transit.*
MEREDITH BROSNAN, *Mr. Dynamite.*
GERALD L. BRUNS,
    Modern Poetry and the Idea of Language.
EVGENY BUNIMOVICH AND J. KATES, EDS.,
    Contemporary Russian Poetry: An Anthology.
GABRIELLE BURTON, *Heartbreak Hotel.*
MICHEL BUTOR, *Degrees.*
    Mobile.
    Portrait of the Artist as a Young Ape.
G. CABRERA INFANTE, *Infante's Inferno.*
    Three Trapped Tigers.
JULIETA CAMPOS, *The Fear of Losing Eurydice.*
ANNE CARSON, *Eros the Bittersweet.*
CAMILO JOSÉ CELA, *Christ versus Arizona.*
    The Family of Pascual Duarte.
    The Hive.
LOUIS-FERDINAND CÉLINE, *Castle to Castle.*
    Conversations with Professor Y.
    London Bridge.
    North.
    Rigadoon.
HUGO CHARTERIS, *The Tide Is Right.*
JEROME CHARYN, *The Tar Baby.*
MARC CHOLODENKO, *Mordechai Schamz.*
EMILY HOLMES COLEMAN, *The Shutter of Snow.*
ROBERT COOVER, *A Night at the Movies.*
STANLEY CRAWFORD, *Some Instructions to My Wife.*
ROBERT CREELEY, *Collected Prose.*
RENÉ CREVEL, *Putting My Foot in It.*
RALPH CUSACK, *Cadenza.*
SUSAN DAITCH, *L.C.*
    Storytown.
NIGEL DENNIS, *Cards of Identity.*
PETER DIMOCK,
    A Short Rhetoric for Leaving the Family.
ARIEL DORFMAN, *Konfidenz.*
COLEMAN DOWELL, *The Houses of Children.*
    Island People.
    Too Much Flesh and Jabez.
RIKKI DUCORNET, *The Complete Butcher's Tales.*
    The Fountains of Neptune.
    The Jade Cabinet.
    Phosphor in Dreamland.
    The Stain.
    The Word "Desire."
WILLIAM EASTLAKE, *The Bamboo Bed.*
    Castle Keep.
    Lyric of the Circle Heart.
JEAN ECHENOZ, *Chopin's Move.*
STANLEY ELKIN, *A Bad Man.*
    Boswell: A Modern Comedy.
    Criers and Kibitzers, Kibitzers and Criers.
    The Dick Gibson Show.
    The Franchiser.
    George Mills.
    The Living End.
    The MacGuffin.
    The Magic Kingdom.
    Mrs. Ted Bliss.
    The Rabbi of Lud.
    Van Gogh's Room at Arles.
ANNIE ERNAUX, *Cleaned Out.*

LAUREN FAIRBANKS, *Muzzle Thyself.*
    Sister Carrie.
LESLIE A. FIEDLER.
    Love and Death in the American Novel.
GUSTAVE FLAUBERT, *Bouvard and Pécuchet.*
FORD MADOX FORD, *The March of Literature.*
JON FOSSE, *Melancholy.*
MAX FRISCH, *I'm Not Stiller.*
    Man in the Holocene.
CARLOS FUENTES, *Christopher Unborn.*
    Distant Relations.
    Terra Nostra.
    Where the Air Is Clear.
JANICE GALLOWAY, *Foreign Parts.*
    The Trick Is to Keep Breathing.
WILLIAM H. GASS, *A Temple of Texts.*
    The Tunnel.
    Willie Masters' Lonesome Wife.
ETIENNE GILSON, *The Arts of the Beautiful.*
    Forms and Substances in the Arts.
C. S. GISCOMBE, *Giscome Road.*
    Here.
DOUGLAS GLOVER, *Bad News of the Heart.*
    The Enamoured Knight.
WITOLD GOMBROWICZ, *A Kind of Testament.*
KAREN ELIZABETH GORDON, *The Red Shoes.*
GEORGI GOSPODINOV, *Natural Novel.*
JUAN GOYTISOLO, *Count Julian.*
    Marks of Identity.
PATRICK GRAINVILLE, *The Cave of Heaven.*
HENRY GREEN, *Blindness.*
    Concluding.
    Doting.
    Nothing.
JIŘÍ GRUŠA, *The Questionnaire.*
GABRIEL GUDDING, *Rhode Island Notebook.*
JOHN HAWKES, *Whistlejacket.*
AIDAN HIGGINS, *A Bestiary.*
    Bornholm Night-Ferry.
    Flotsam and Jetsam.
    Langrishe, Go Down.
    Scenes from a Receding Past.
    Windy Arbours.
ALDOUS HUXLEY, *Antic Hay.*
    Crome Yellow.
    Point Counter Point.
    Those Barren Leaves.
    Time Must Have a Stop.
MIKHAIL IOSSEL AND JEFF PARKER, EDS., *Amerika:*
    Contemporary Russians View
    the United States.
GERT JONKE, *Geometric Regional Novel.*
JACQUES JOUET, *Mountain R.*
HUGH KENNER, *The Counterfeiters.*
    Flaubert, Joyce and Beckett:
    The Stoic Comedians.
    Joyce's Voices.
DANILO KIŠ, *Garden, Ashes.*
    A Tomb for Boris Davidovich.
AIKO KITAHARA,
    The Budding Tree: Six Stories of Love in Edo.
ANITA KONKKA, *A Fool's Paradise.*
GEORGE KONRÁD, *The City Builder.*
TADEUSZ KONWICKI, *A Minor Apocalypse.*
    The Polish Complex.
MENIS KOUMANDAREAS, *Koula.*
ELAINE KRAF, *The Princess of 72nd Street.*
JIM KRUSOE, *Iceland.*
EWA KURYLUK, *Century 21.*
VIOLETTE LEDUC, *La Bâtarde.*
DEBORAH LEVY, *Billy and Girl.*
    Pillow Talk in Europe and Other Places.
JOSÉ LEZAMA LIMA, *Paradiso.*
ROSA LIKSOM, *Dark Paradise.*
OSMAN LINS, *Avalovara.*
    The Queen of the Prisons of Greece.
ALF MAC LOCHLAINN, *The Corpus in the Library.*
    Out of Focus.
RON LOEWINSOHN, *Magnetic Field(s).*
D. KEITH MANO, *Take Five.*
BEN MARCUS, *The Age of Wire and String.*
WALLACE MARKFIELD, *Teitlebaum's Window.*
    To an Early Grave.
DAVID MARKSON, *Reader's Block.*
    Springer's Progress.
    Wittgenstein's Mistress.
CAROLE MASO, *AVA.*

FOR A FULL LIST OF PUBLICATIONS, VISIT:
www.dalkeyarchive.com

SELECTED DALKEY ARCHIVE PAPERBACKS

FOR A FULL LIST OF PUBLICATIONS, VISIT:
w w w . d a l k e y a r c h i v e . c o m